Anonymous

Questions, Diagrams and Illustrations for Analytic Study and Recitation

Anatiposi

Anonymous

Questions, Diagrams and Illustrations for Analytic Study and Recitation

Reprint of the original, first published in 1871.

1st Edition 2023 | ISBN: 978-3-38211-282-0

Anatiposi Verlag is an imprint of Outlook Verlagsgesellschaft mbH.

Verlag (Publisher): Outlook Verlag GmbH, Zeilweg 44, 60439 Frankfurt, Deutschland
Vertretungsberechtigt (Authorized to represent): E. Roepke, Zeilweg 44, 60439 Frankfurt, Deutschland
Druck (Print): Books on Demand GmbH, In de Tarpen 42, 22848 Norderstedt, Deutschland

QUESTIONS,

DIAGRAMS AND ILLUSTRATIONS

FOR

Analytic Study and Recitation.

ALSO FOR

UNIFIC AND SYNTHETIC REVIEW OF

CUTTER'S NEW ANALYTIC ANATOMY,

PHYSIOLOGY AND HYGIENE,

HUMAN AND COMPARATIVE.

PHILADELPHIA:

J. B. LIPPINCOTT & CO.

SCHOOL TEXT-BOOKS.

Sanford's Higher Analytical Arithmetic; or,

The Method of Making Arithmetical Calculations on Principles of Universal Application, without the Aid of Formal Rules. By SHELTON P. SANFORD, A.M. 12mo. 419 pp. $1.50.

"I have examined Prof. Sanford's Analytical Arithmetic, and have no hesitation in saying, in general terms, that I have no doubt it is the best book of the kind *in the world*. Many attempts have been made to reduce the science of numbers to its last analysis, but so far as I know or believe this is the only attempt that has completely succeeded. I am satisfied that it ought to supersede all other books of its class."—H. H. TUCKER, *Prest. of Mercer University, Ga., and Prest. of the Ga. Teachers' Association.*

"PHILADELPHIA, June 27, 1870.

"Sanford's Analytical Arithmetic possesses the three-fold advantage of clear and correct definitions, of well-illustrated rules, and of a judicious arrangement of the whole subject. This work will hold a high place in the estimation of educators who desire to combine mental training and the imparting of an accurate knowledge of the most useful of the exact sciences." — JAMES McCLUNE, *Prof. of Mathematics and Astronomy in Philadelphia Central High School.*

Sanford's Intermediate Analytical Arithmetic.

By SHELTON P. SANFORD, A.M. 16mo. 232 pp. 50 cents.

"The work here presented is preliminary to the Author's larger 'Analytical Arithmetic,' and is intended to make the pupil, by easy and uniform steps, expert in the use of figures, and at the same time to teach him the *reason* of each operation. Apart from the knowledge of Arithmetic, the Author believes that the habitudes of thought engendered by the study of the Analytic System will prove of inestimable value to the student in every department of practical and professional life."—*Extract from the Author's Preface.*

Sanford's First Lessons in Analytical Arithmetic. (In press.)

Wickersham's School Economy. A Treatise on

the Preparation, Organization, Employments, Government and Authorities of Schools. By J. P. WICKERSHAM, A.M., *Pennsylvania State Supt. of Common Schools.* Second edition. 12mo. Cloth. $1.50.

Wickersham's Methods of Instruction; or, That

Part of the Philosophy of Education which Treats of the Nature of the Several Branches of Knowledge and the Method of Teaching them. By J. P. WICKERSHAM, A.M., *Pennsylvania State Superintendent of Common Schools.* 12mo. Cloth. $1.75.

J. B. LIPPINCOTT & CO., Publishers,

715 and 717 Market St., Philadelphia.

ANALYSIS OF CONTENTS.

DIVISION I.
OUTLINE PRINCIPLES.
CHAPTER I.—GENERAL REMARKS.

DIVISION II.
MOTORY APPARATUS.
CHAPTER IV.—THE BONES.

DIVISION III.
NUTRITIVE APPARATUS.
CHAPTER VI.—THE DIGESTIVE ORGANS.

For Treatment of Wounds, see ¶ 363. For Recovery of Drowned Persons, see ¶ 430. For Treatment of Burns, see ¶ 610. For Treatment of Frost-Bite, see ¶ 612.

QUESTIONS, DIAGRAMS AND ILLUSTRATIONS

FOR ANALYTICAL STUDY AND RECITATION,

ALSO FOR UNIFIC AND SYNTHETIC REVIEW OF

CUTTER'S ANALYTIC ANATOMY, PHYSIOLOGY AND HYGIENE,

HUMAN AND COMPARATIVE.

PROFITABLE *reading* and *study* require the same analysis and method as clear and efficient *teaching*. *Unification* of ideas and principles is also aided by varied and frequent reviews.

To aid *pupil* and *teacher*, the following *Questions, Diagrams* and *Illustrations* have been prepared. The Questions in the larger type are to be used in the *analytic study* and *recitation of paragraphs;* those in the smaller type, to aid pupil and teacher to secure *unific* investigation and review of parts more or less *analogous* in *structure, function* or *hygiene;* while the diagrams and illustrations are to be used in *synthetical* examination and review of the sections, chapters and divisions.

I would also suggest the use of the blackboard in drawing outline figures and diagrams, and in writing the topics to be reviewed.

DIVISION I.—OUTLINE PRINCIPLES.

ANALYTIC EXAMINATION.

CHAPTER I.—GENERAL REMARKS.

§ 1. *The Three Kingdoms of Nature Compared.*

1. State the Linnæan distinctions of the three kingdoms of Nature. Name the three kingdoms, and define each.
2. Of what are Organic and Inorganic bodies combinations? What is said respecting Life-force?
3. Give the distinguishing features of Organized and Unorganized matter.
4. State the distinctions between animals and plants.
5. What is said of these distinctions in the lower forms of life?

.§ 2. *Definition of Terms.*

6. Define Organ, Apparatus and Function. What is Anatomy? Physiology? Hygiene?
7. Of what are organs composed? Define Histology and Chemistry.

CHAPTER II.—GENERAL HISTOLOGY.

§ 3. *Cells.*

8. Where do you find Unity of Plan?
9. Define Protoplasm. What is Animal Protoplasm?
10. What is said of nucleated cells? Of the vital functions of these cells?
11. Distinguish between animal and vegetable cells.
12. Of what is the simple cell the type?
13. Of what does a simple cell consist? Give an illustration.
14. To what modifications are cells subject?
15. What is the shape of the cells?
16. In what ways do cells multiply?
17. What is said of the growth and decay of cells?

§ 4. *Primary Tissues.*

18. How are the different tissues of the body formed? Upon what do their characters depend?
19. To what are the Primary Tissues reducible?

20. State the object and character of the Connective Tissues.
21. Of what is the Fibrous form composed? State its nature and forms.
22. Give the composition and forms of the White Fibrous tissue. What is Gelatin?
23. Describe the Yellow Fibrous tissue. Why called Elastic? Does it gelatinize? Where found? When found together, what proportion of White to Yellow Fibrous tissue? Observation.
24. Of what does the Areolar form consist? What is said of its cellular structure? What of its individuality? Observation.
25. Describe the Cartilaginous tissue. Mention the properties of Cartilage. Where is this tissue found? What is the relation of cartilage to bone?
26. Under what condition is Fibro-cartilage formed? State quality and adaptation.
27. What peculiarity has the Adipose tissue? Of what composed? Where found? Its use?
28. Where is the Sclerous tissue found? What is said of its composition?
29. Give the composition of Muscular tissue. Name its kinds, and describe each. What is its characteristic? What of its electrical nature?
30. Describe the Tubular tissue. What is the office of the capillary vessels? Of what are their walls composed? Where is this tissue found?
31. How is the Nervous tissue distinguished? Where found? In what respect like the Muscular tissue? Mention its elements.
32. Describe the Ganglionic Corpuscles.
33. What is said of the Gray fibres? Where found?
34. Speak of the White fibres.
35. Where are the gray and white substances found?

₰ 5. *Membranes.*

36. What is the Basement membrane? Why so called?
37. Name and describe the varieties of the Epithelium. Of what power the Cilia? Where is the Ciliated Epithelium found?
38. What is beneath the basement membrane? What are constituted by the epithelium, basement membrane, and fibro-areolar tissue?
39. Where is the Serous membrane found? Its qualities?

1 *

40. What is said of the Synovial membrane? Observation.
41. Describe the Mucous membranes.
42. Where is the Gastro-Pulmonary Mucous membrane found?
43. Where the Urinary?
44. What is continuous with the Mucous membrane? Observation.

CHAPTER III.—GENERAL CHEMISTRY.

§ 6. *Solids and Fluids.*

45. Of what is the human body composed? What is said of the proportion of solids and fluids?
46. What are Proximate Constituents? Define Organic and Inorganic Proximate Constituents.
47. Name the Inorganic Proximate Constituents.
48. Give the classes of Organic Proximate Constituents.
49. What are contained in the Nitrogenous class? Name the most important.
50. What is the office of Albumen in the animal economy? Give the derivation of its name. Where found? What peculiarity has it?
51. Describe Albuminose.
52. What is Fibrin? Where found? What is the influence of alcohol upon it?
53. Describe Musculin. How hardened?
54. Where is Globulin and Hæmatin found?
55. Give the properties of Casein. Where does it exist?
56. Define Cartilagin. What is Osteine? Chondrigen?
57. Define and give the property of Salivin.
58. Describe Pepsin, and state its property.
59. What is Pancreatin? and state its actions.
60. Describe Mucin.
61. What is Neurin?
62. Define Keratin.
63. To what is Elastin peculiar?
64. Where is Melanin found?
65. Of what use Biliverdin? Color?
66. Name the acids of the nitrogenous class.
67. Mention the non-nitrogenous group.
68. Of what are the fats composed? From what derived? What is Glycerine?
69. Mention the different kinds of sugars. Where are starch granules found?

70. Name the ultimate chemical elements, with their percentage proportions.
71. In what condition are oxygen and hydrogen? What is said of carbon?
72. What becomes of the chemical elements in decomposition?

UNIFIC REVIEW.

[Compare 9 with 119.]
What is the relation of Protoplasm to ossification?

[Compare 11–17 with 119, 120, 152, 173, 174, 237, 306, 335, 339, 340, 378, 389, 458, 464, 465, 547 and 553–556.]
Where do you find nucleated cells? Have they any influence on the plan of structure? What relation does the cellular tissue bear to the muscular? In the lining of what organs do you find epithelial cells? In the lining membranes of what organs do you find ciliated epithelium? What is said of the nucleated cells in the nervous tissue?

[Compare 20–26 with 123–126, 177, 306, 334–340, 387, 388, 463 and 464.]
Name the connective tissues. Mention some distinguishing features of each. Where do you find the white fibrous tissues? Where the yellow fibrous? Where is cartilage found?

[Compare 28 with 120–122.]
What tissue is found in the bones?

[Compare 29 with 173–176, 240–243, 306 and 337–340.]
What is the structure of muscular tissue? Where found?

[Compare 30, 341 with 459–462.]
In what blood-vessels do you find the tubular tissue? In what system?

[Compare 31–35 with 457–462.]
Tell what you can about the nervous tissue.

[Compare 36–38 with 237, 238, 240–243, 246, 335, 339, 340, 376–379, 388, 389, 463 and 464.]
Name the parts of the body where you find the Basement membrane.

[Compare 39 with 246, 334, 390 and 463.]
Where is the Serous membrane found?

[Compare 40 with 125 and 177.]
What is the office of the Synovial membrane?

[Compare 41–44 with 237, 238, 240–243, 386–389, 547 and 548.]
Name the Mucous membranes. The mucous membrane lines what organs? Point out the difference between mucous and serous membranes. With what is the mucous membrane continuous?

FIG. 191.

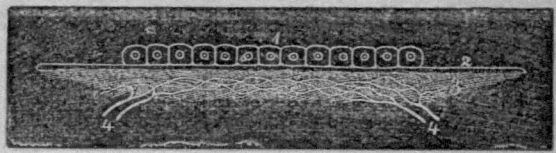

FIG. 191 (*Leidy*). DIAGRAM EXHIBITING THE RELATIVE POSITION OF THE COMMON ANA-
TOMICAL ELEMENTS OF SEROUS AND MUCOUS MEMBRANES, THE GLANDS, THE LUNGS AND
THE SKIN.—1, Epithelium, secreting cells or epidermis, composed of nucleated cells, and
occupying the free surface of the structure mentioned. 2, Basement layer, represented
much thicker than natural, in comparison with the other layers. 3, Fibrous layer, in
which the arteries and veins (4, 4) terminate in a capillary network. Magnified.

FIG. 192

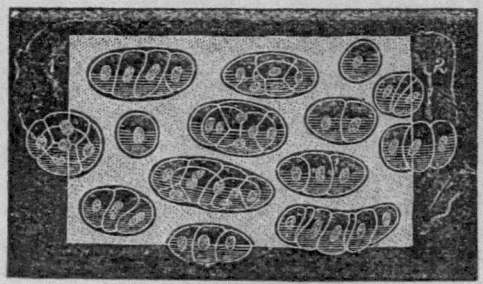

FIG. 193.

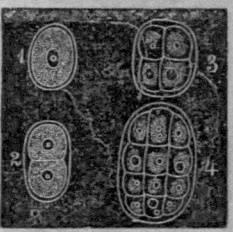

FIG. 192 (*Leidy*). CARTILAGE.—Section through the thickness of the oval cartilage of
the nose. 1, Toward the exterior. 2, Toward the interior surface; highly magnified.
It exhibits groups of cartilage cells imbedded in a homogeneous matrice.

FIG. 193 (*Leidy*). PROCESS OF MULTIPLICATION, or CARTILAGE CELLS.—1, Simple cartilage
cell from the embryo. 2, Increase of cartilage cells by division of the primary cell. 3, 4,
Groups of cartilage cells, from an adult articular cartilage. Magnified.

FIG. 194.

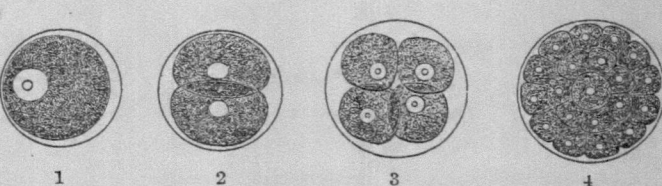

1   2   3   4

FIG. 194 (*Leidy*). AN IDEAL CELL.—1, Cell with its wall, protoplasm, nucleus and its
nucleolus. 2, The same divided into two. 3, The same divided into four cells. 4, The
same divided into many cells. The dark portion, the protoplasm; the white spot, the
nucleus; the inner small circle, the nucleolus. Magnified.

SYNTHETIC REVIEW.

Essential distinctions between mineral, vegetable and animal kingdoms,
Nature of life-force,
Vitalized and non-vitalized bodies compared,
Animals and plants compared,
These distinctions in higher and lower forms.

§ 1. *Three Kingdoms compared.*

Organ, apparatus and functions,
Anatomy, Physiology and Hygiene,
Structure of organs,
Histology and Chemistry.

§ 2. *Definition of Terms.*

CHAP. I. *General Remarks.*

Unity of plan in animals and plants,
Protoplasm,
Nucleated cell,
Simple cell,
Adaptation to different offices,
Life and shape of cells,
Modes of multiplication of cells,
Growth, perfection and decay,
Primary tissues,
Object of the connective tissue.

§ 3. *Cells.*

Fibrous tissue,
Areolar,
Cartilaginous,
Adipose,
Sclerous,
Muscular,
Tubular,
Nervous.

§ 4. *Primary Tissues.*

CHAP. II. *General Histology.*

Basement membrane,
Epithelium,
Serous membrane,
Synovial "
Mucous membranes.

§ 5. *Membranes.*

Solids and fluids,
Proximate constituents,
Inorganic "
Organic "
Nitrogenous "
Non-nitrogenous "
Ultimate chemical elements.

§ 6. *Solids and Fluids.*

CHAP. III. *General Chemistry.*

Division I. *Outline Principles.*

State the General Remarks, the General Histology and the General Chemistry of the human system.

A *

DIVISION II.—THE MOTORY APPARATUS.

ANALYTIC EXAMINATION.

73. Why is the Motory Apparatus so called? Name its organs.

CHAPTER IV.—THE BONES.

§ 7. Anatomy of the Bones.

74. Of what does the Internal Framework of the body consist?
75. State the number and classes of the bones.
76. Name the bones of the Head.
77. How many bones compose the Skull? Give their names and positions.
78. What is said of the skull-bones? How are they united? Observation.
79. How many bones in the Face? Name and describe them.
80. The Ear has how many bones?
81. State the number and names of the bones of the Trunk.
82. How is the Thorax formed? What its natural form? What organs does it contain?
83. What is the situation of the Sternum?
84. Describe the Ribs. Distinguish between true and false. Why the floating ribs so called? What of their length and breadth?
85. Of what is the Spinal Column composed? What is meant by body and process of a vertebra? State their uses. What is said of the arrangement of these processes?
86. State the arrangement of the Vertebræ.
87. Describe the Cervical vertebræ.
88. What is said of the Dorsal?
89. How are the Lumbar distinguished?
90. What is found upon the Anterior and Posterior parts of the vertebræ?
91. What are found between the arches of the vertebræ? How do they differ from other ligaments?
92. Speak of the Intervertebral ligaments.
93. Of what is the Pelvis composed?
94. Describe the Innominatum.
95. What is the Sacrum?
96. What changes occur in the Coccyx during life?

97. Mention the number and names of the bones of the Upper Extremities.
98. Where is the Scapula situated?
99. To what is the Clavicle attached?
100. Describe the Humerus. What cavity in this bone?
101. What is the Ulna?
102. What is the position of the Radius? With what does it articulate?
103. Speak of the number and arrangement of the bones of the Carpus.
104. State the arrangement of the Metacarpal bones.
105. How many bones in the phalanges of the fingers?
106. How many in the Lower Extremities? What their names?
107. What is said of the Femur?
108. Patella?
109. Tibia?
110. Fibula?
111. Tarsus?
112. Of how many bones does the Metatarsus consist?
113. How many do the phalanges of the toes contain?
114. How are joints formed? Name their groups.
115. Mention and describe each kind of immovable joints.
116. What are the mixed joints? Give examples.
117. What is said of movable joints? How many kinds? Describe each.
118. Give special description of certain forms of movable joints.

§ 8. *Histology of the Bones.*

119. What is the character of the primitive basis of bone? State the changes previous to ossification.
120. Give the Intra-cartilaginous mode of ossification.
121. State the Intra-membranous mode.
122. What are the structure and texture of the long bones? Where is the Medulla found?
123. Distinguish between the Periosteum and Endosteum.
124. Of what service is Cartilage? How arranged?
125. Of what use the Synovial membrane? Name and describe its kinds.
126. What are found in connection with the Synovial membrane? Describe the several kinds of ligaments.

§ 9. *Chemistry of the Bones.*

127. Of what are the bones composed? Mention the mineral constituents. Observation.

§ 10. *Physiology of the Bones.*

128. Name the uses of the Bones.
129. What qualities found in bone?
130. What advantages result from the structure and arrangement of the skull-bones?
131. Mention the offices of the spinal column.
132. How are strength and firmness secured? How the necessary rotary movement? To what are the muscles attached? What arrangement for the spinal cord? What provision is made to prevent injury to the brain?
133. What purpose do the Ribs serve?
134. State the offices of the Pelvis.
135. What is said of the form and proportion of the Upper Extremities as relating to the hand?
136. Compare the Lower Extremities with the Upper.
137. Why are the shafts of the long bones hollow?
138. Enumerate the uses of the joints.
139. State the purposes of the different classes of joints.
140. Give the use of the Synovia.
141. What is said of Cartilage?
142. Speak of the function of the Ligaments.
143. Of what service the Periosteum?
144. What is illustrated by each bone?

§ 11. *Hygiene of the Bones.*

145. What is the influence of exercise on the health of the bones? How should it be taken?
146. To what are the lower extremities of the very young not adapted?
147. What should be avoided? Why?
148. Why should an erect position be maintained?
149. How are distortions of the body produced?
150. What statements by eminent physicians? How may slight curvatures of the spine be prevented or cured?
151. In the fracture of bones or injury of limbs, what is necessary? What is "White Swelling?" Observation.

§ **12.** *Comparative Osteology*

152. Name and describe the sub-kingdoms.
153. Give the classes of the Vertebrata.
154. Compare the Vertebral Column of Mammals. What is said of it in Birds? Reptiles? Fishes?
155. What is said of the bones of the head in Mammals? Birds? Reptiles? Fishes?
156. Why not a Clavicle in the ox. Describe the clavicle of Birds. Reptiles. Fishes.
157. What of the Scapula of the lower order of animals?
158. Speak of the Sternum of Birds. Reptiles. Fishes.
159. Describe the Ribs in the different classes.
160. What is said of the Humerus?
161. What of the Radius and Ulna?
162. What of the Carpus and Metacarpus?
163. Compare Posterior and Anterior Extremities of the several classes. What suggestion by the author?

UNIFIC REVIEW.

[Compare 74 with 152.]

What constitutes the Skeleton? What is said of it in the different sub-kingdoms?

[Compare 76–79 with 155.]

Compare the Bones of the Head in man with those of the lower animals.

[Compare 81–97 with 154, 158 and 159.]

What are the bones of the Trunk? Are they all found in the lower animals? Which is the largest bone in a Bird?

[Compare 97–106 with 160–162.]

Name all the bones of the Upper Extremities in the different classes of the Vertebrata. What peculiarity in the clavicle of Birds?

[Compare 106–113 with 163.]

Describe each bone of the Lower Extremities.

[Compare 119–122 with 8–11 and 152.]

What is the earliest organic form of living things? State the process of ossification.

[Compare 123 with 21–24.]

What tissue in the Periosteum? Use of this membrane?

[Compare 126 with 21–23.]

What tissue forms the Ligaments?   What does Ligament signify?

[Compare 127 with 47, 52, 56 and 70.]

Name both the organic and inorganic matter in bones.

[Compare 145 with 202, 213, 214, 281, 361 and 506.]

What is necessary to the health of the bones?   What results follow a want of exercise?   State the influence of exercise upon the health of the different organs.

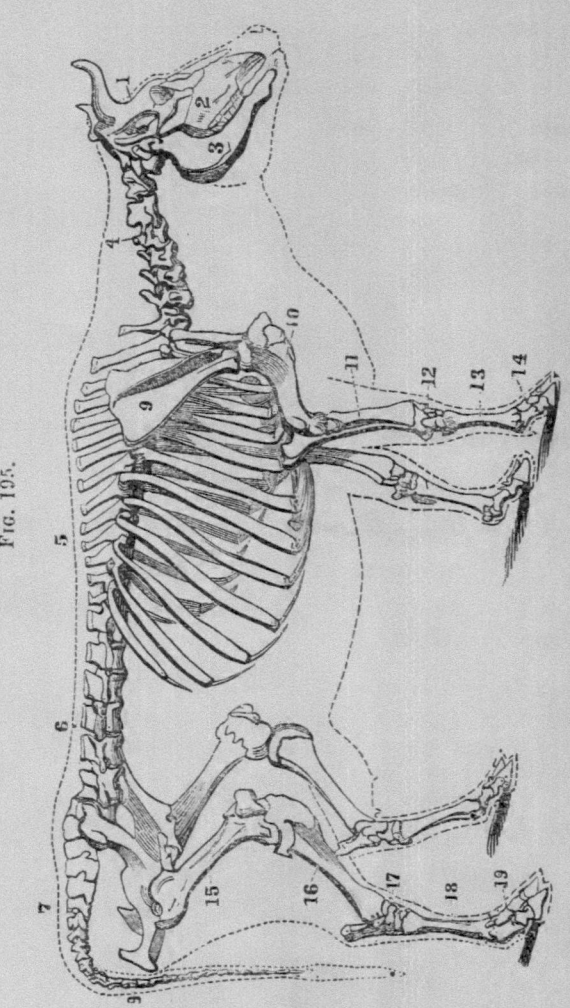

FIG. 195.

FIG. 195. SKELETON OF THE COW.—1, Frontal bone of the head. 2, Upper jaw (superior maxillary). 3, Lower jaw (inferior maxillary). 4, Cervical vertebræ. 5, Dorsal vertebræ. 6, Lumbar vertebræ. 7, Sacral vertebræ. 8, Caudal vertebræ. 9, Scapula. 10, Humerus. 11, Radius and ulna. 12, Carpus. 13, Metacarpus. 14, Phalanges (toes). 15, Femur. 16, Tibia. 17, Tarsus. 18, Metatarsus. 19, Phalanges. In this fig. the same terms are used as for the corresponding bones in man (see fig. 196). The common names vary.

FIG. 196.

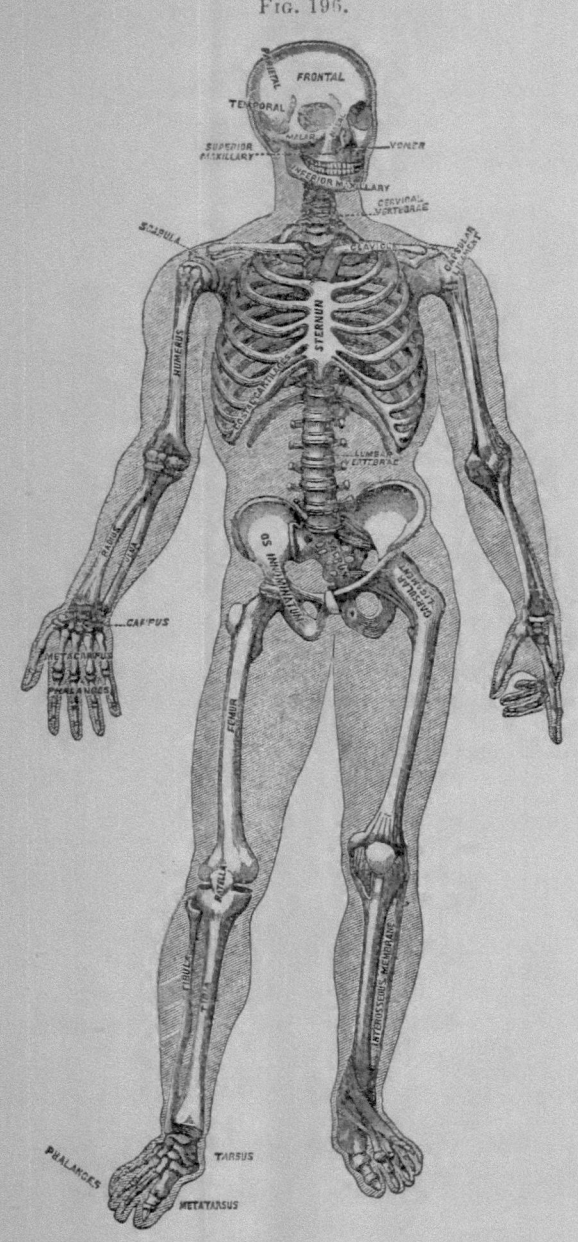

SYNTHETIC REVIEW.

The Skeleton and its uses,	
Number and classes,	
Head, Trunk,	
Upper Extremities,	
Lower Extremities,	§ 7.
Joints,	*Anatomy of.*
Definition and classes of Joints,	
Immovable Joints,	
Mixed, Movable,	
Peculiar forms of Movable.	
Formation of Temporary Cartilage,	
Intra-cartilaginous mode of ossification,	
Intra-membranous mode,	§ 8.
Structure of the Long Bones,	*Histology of.*
Periosteum, Endosteum,	
Cartilages of the Joints,	
Synovial membrane, Ligaments.	
Chemical Composition,	§ 9.
Experiment showing earthy and animal matter.	*Chemistry of.*
General uses of,	
Adaptation of their structure to their uses,	
Skill as shown in the Skull,	
" " Spinal Column,	
" " Ribs,	
" " Pelvis,	
" " Upper Extremities,	
" " Lower Extremities,	§ 10.
" " Long Bones,	*Physiology of*
The uses of the Joints,	
Classification of the Joints,	
Of Movable Joints,	
Function of the Synovia,	
" Cartilages,	
" Ligaments,	
" Periosteum,	
Perfection of this part in the animal fabric.	
Effect of exercise upon the bones of children,	
" compression,	
" stooping,	§ 11.
Treatment of Fractures,	*Hygiene of.*
" Sprains,	
" Felons.	
Classification of Animals,	
" Vertebrates,	
Compare Spinal Column of Vertebrates,	§ 12.
" Bones of the Head,	*Comparative Osteology of.*
" " Thorax,	
" " Extremities.	

CHAP. IV.
The Bones.

Give the Human and Comparative Anatomy and Histology of the Bones; the Chemistry, the Physiology and the Hygiene.

ANALYTIC EXAMINATION.

CHAPTER V.—THE MUSCLES.

§ 13. *Anatomy of the Muscles.*

164. What property do the Muscles possess? By what law governed? Give the different forms.
165. Describe the Fasciæ. Define Origin and Insertion.
166. Give the number and kinds of the muscles.
167. How arranged? Define Extensors and Flexors.
168. State the office of the Occipito-Frontalis; of the Orbicularis Palpebrarum; of the Orbicularis Oris; of the Masseter and Temporal; of the Sterno-Cleido-Mastoid.
169. Of the Pectoralis Major; of the Serratus Magnus; of the Obliquus Externus and Rectus Abdominalis.
170. Of the Trapezius, Rhomboideus Major and Minor; of the Latissimus Dorsi; of the Serratus Posticus Inferior.
171. Of the Deltoid; of the Biceps; of the Triceps; of the Flexor Carpi Radialis; of the Flexor Carpi Ulnaris; of the Flexor Digitorum; of the Extensor Digitorum; of the Extensor Carpi Radialis.
172. Describe the Glutei, Sartorius, Rectus Femoris, Vastus Externus, Vastus Internus, Triceps Abductor Femoris, Biceps Femoris, Extensor Digitorum, Peroneus Longus, Gastrochnemius Externus, Tendo-Achilles.

§ 14. *Histology of the Muscles.*

173. Into what is a Muscle separable?
174. By what is each muscle invested? What is Myolemma?
175. Name and describe the classes of muscles.
176. How is the contractility of the muscles stimulated?
177. What are Tendons? In what is each tendon enveloped?
178. Where do you find the blood-vessels of the muscles?
179. What position do the Nerves occupy? What is said of the different classes of the nerves?

§ 15. *Chemistry of the Muscles.*

180. What is said of the chemical composition of the muscles? Muscle sugar is where found?
181. How does proper muscular substance differ from simple fibrous tissue?

2 *

182. Name some of the chemical changes attending muscular action. What is said of the "muscular current"? Observation.

§ 16. *Physiology of the Muscles.*

183. State the relative uses of bones and muscles.
184. Name the uses of the muscles.
185. To what are the Voluntary muscles subject? What is implied by the motion of a limb?
186. Of what aid the muscular sense? What is said of the exercise of this muscular sense?
187. What are the Involuntary muscles?
188. What involuntary muscles are somewhat under the control of the Will? Of what advantage this? Observation.
189. State the office of the Tendons. Do they possess contractility? In what respect do you see in them an exhibition of care and skill? Illustrate with the hand.
190. Define a Lever, and name its kinds.
191. Explain each kind.
192. Where are the principles of the first kind illustrated?
193. Where those of the second?
194. Of the third?
195. What is said of the oblique action of the muscles? What is important to notice in this connection? Compare the Extensors with the Flexors.
196. Where does the pulley find illustration?
197. What is said of the direction of the different layers?
198. In what is mechanical skill shown?
199. Speak of muscular force.

§ 17. *Hygiene of the Muscles.*

200. What advantage in possessing healthy muscles? Name the first essential. What is the influence of pure blood on the muscles?
201. Why should the muscles not be compressed? What is said of the pressure of dressing in case of a fractured limb? What are the results of tight dresses on health? To what is tight-lacing compared?
202. How does exercise promote the health and growth of muscles? Illustration.
203. State the relation of relaxation to contraction. Illustration.

204. Give a reason for a change of employment. Illustration.
205. How should the muscles be called into action? Observation.
206. How rested?
207. How should exercise be taken?
208. What kind of exercise? What pastimes should be chosen?
209. To what should the amount of exercise be adapted? Observation.
210. State the proper time for exercise. Observation.
211. Mention the influence of the mind on the muscles.
212. What should be taken into consideration as to the amount of exercise?
213. In what diseases are great care and discretion necessary as regards exercise?
214. What is said of the exercise of the muscles in chronic diseases of the digestive organs? What is important to secure beneficial results? Observation.
215. Why do the muscles require erect positions of the body?
216. What attention should be given to children and youth? What care in furnishing school-rooms? Observation.
217. Why relaxation of muscles necessary in walking, jumping, etc.? Observation.
218. State and illustrate the influence of education. Observation.

₰ 18. *Comparative Myology.*

219. What is said of the muscles of Mammals? Of their color?
220. For what is the muscular system of Birds remarkable?
221. Speak of the muscles of Reptiles.
222. What modification of muscles in Fishes? What color?

UNIFIC REVIEW.

[Compare 164, 165, 166 with 173, 174 and 219–222.]
What is the structure of the muscles? State their relation to the bones. Compare the muscles of man with those of other mammals. What is peculiar to muscle?

[Compare 176 with 441, 450 and 469.]
What are the causes of muscular activity? State the connection between the muscular and nervous system.

[Compare 177 with 22.]
Where do you find the white fibrous and muscular tissue closely related?

[Compare 178 with 371.]
How are the muscles nourished?

[Compare 180 with 50–54.]

Of what is the muscular tissue composed?

[Compare 201 with 360 and 425.]

State the evil results of compression of the muscles.

[Compare 202 with 361 and 506.]

What is the influence of exercise on circulation and muscular power?
What the effect of a want of it on the Nervous System?

[Compare 203 with 209, 210, 281 and 506.]

In taking exercise, what caution as to the age, time, amount, etc.?

FIG. 197.

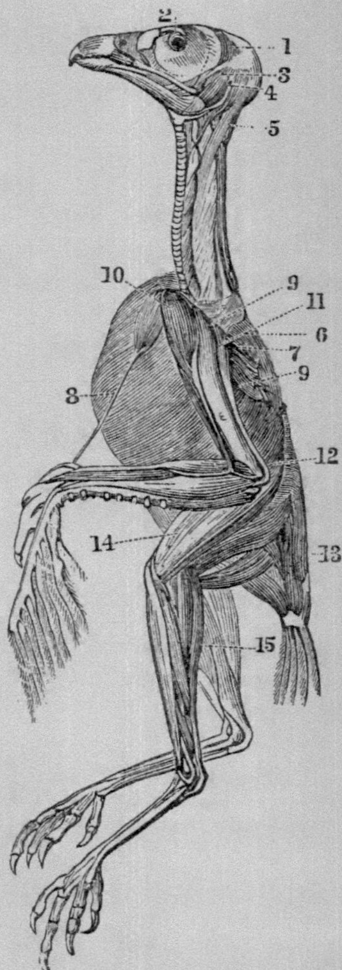

FIG. 198. SUPERFICIAL MUSCLES OF A HAWK.—1, Occipito-Frontalis. 2, Orbicularis Palpebrarum. 3, Temporal. 4, Masseter. 5, Sterno-cleido-Mastoid. 6, Trapezius. 7, Latissimus Dorsi. 8, Pectoralis. 9, Deltoid. 10, Biceps. 11, Triceps. 12, Glutæi. 13, Levator Caudæ. 14, Rectus Femoris. 15, Gastrocnemius muscle.

SYNTHETIC REVIEW.

Law of muscular contraction,
Consequent forms of muscles,
Modes of attachment,
Number and general arrangement,
Of Head and Neck,
" Anterior part of Trunk,
" Posterior "
" Upper Extremities,
" Lower Extremities.

§ 13.
Anatomy of.

Analysis,
Sheaths,
Voluntary and involuntary,
Exciting agents of contractility,
Tendons,
Blood-vessels,
Nerves.

§ 14.
Histology of.

Chemical composition,
Chemical changes attending muscular action,
Muscular current.

§ 15.
Chemistry of.

Relative uses of Bones and Muscles,
Important functions,
Relation of the Will to muscular action,
" " muscular sense " "
The muscular sense a source of enjoyment,
Importance of involuntary movements,
Importance of such movements being some-
   times voluntary,
Tendons,
Mechanical powers exhibited in muscular
   action,
Lever, Pulley,
Oblique action, etc.,
Deep-seated,
Minute.

§ 16.
*Physiology
of.*

CHAP. V.
The Muscles.

Healthy condition,
Freedom from compression,
Exercise,
Conditions to be observed in exercise,
Exercise sometimes injurious,
Effect of mental stimulus,
Regard necessary to age and health,
Position of the body,
Proper tension,
Education.

§ 17.
Hygiene of.

Muscles of other mammals and man,
" Birds,
" Reptiles,
" Fishes.

§ 18.
*Comparative
Myology of.*

Give the Anatomy, the Histology, the Chemistry, the Physiology,
the Hygiene, Human and Comparative, of the Muscles.

Fig. 198.

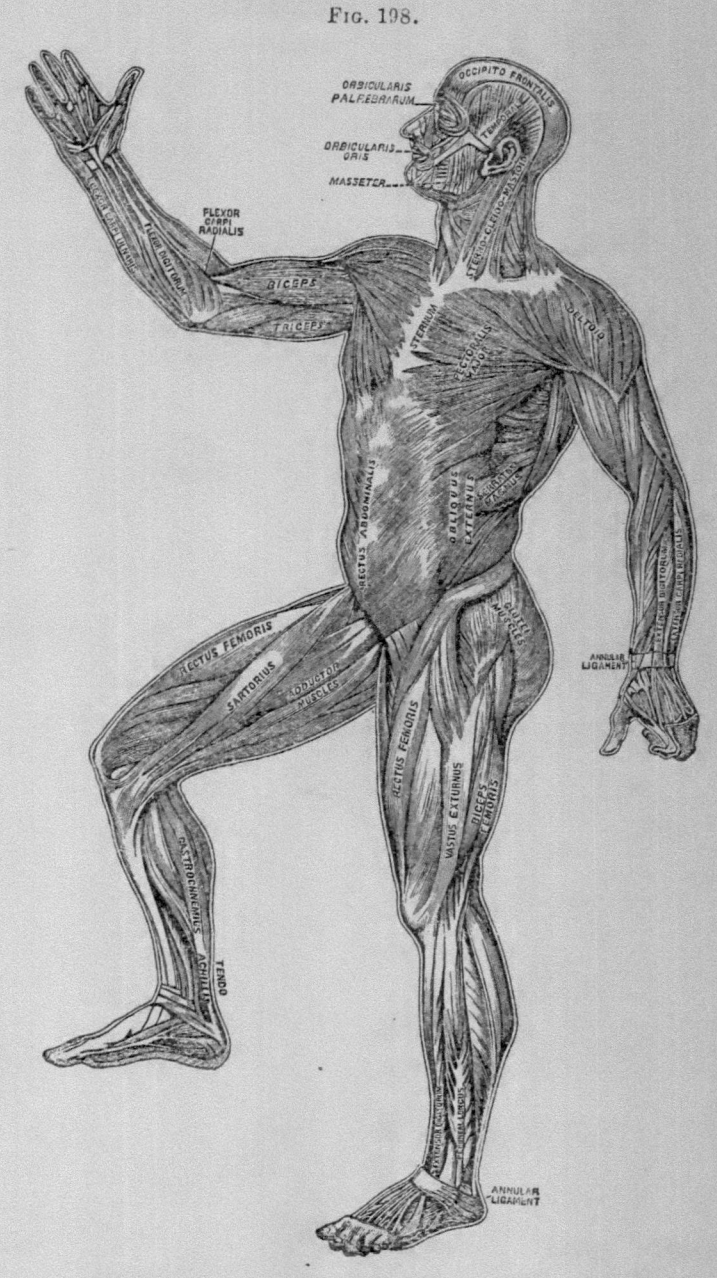

DIVISION II.—MOTORY APPARATUS.

SYNTHETIC REVIEW.

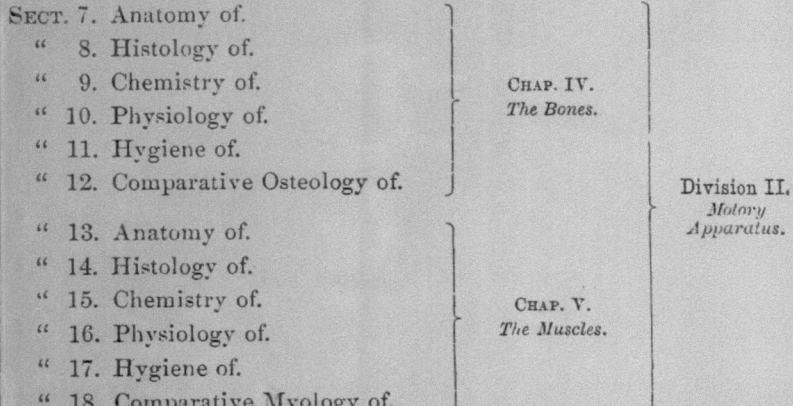

Sect. 7. Anatomy of.
" 8. Histology of.
" 9. Chemistry of.   CHAP. IV.
" 10. Physiology of.   *The Bones.*
" 11. Hygiene of.
" 12. Comparative Osteology of.
                                                Division II.
" 13. Anatomy of.   *Motory*
" 14. Histology of.   *Apparatus.*
" 15. Chemistry of.   CHAP. V.
" 16. Physiology of.   *The Muscles.*
" 17. Hygiene of.
" 18. Comparative Myology of.

Give the Anatomy, the Histology, the Chemistry, the Physiology, the Hygiene, Human and Comparative, of the Motory Apparatus.

DIVISION III.—THE NUTRITIVE APPARATUS.

ANALYTIC EXAMINATION.

223. In what processes are the organs of the Nutritive Apparatus used? Name the organs.

CHAPTER VI.—THE DIGESTIVE ORGANS.

§ 19. *Anatomy of the Digestive Organs.*

224. What are included in the Digestive Organs?
225. Describe the Mouth.
226. What is said of the Teeth? How many parts has each tooth? Observation.
227. What are the temporary teeth? The permanent? Name and describe the different forms of the teeth.
228. Of how many pairs do the Salivary Glands consist? Name and describe each pair. Observation.
229. Describe the Pharynx.
230. What is the Œsophagus?
231. What is said of the Stomach?
232. Mention the divisions of the Intestines. Describe the small intestine.
233. State the length and parts of the large intestine. Describe each part.
234. Describe the Liver. By what surrounded? How many lobes? What is on the under side?
235. What is said of the Pancreas?
236. What is the Spleen? Why so named?

§ 20. *Histoloyy of the Digestive Organs.*

237. By what is the alimentary canal lined?
238. Describe the covering of the mouth. Describe the tongue. Name and describe its muscles. Distinguish between hard and soft palate.
239. What is the relation of the teeth to the mucous membrane of the mouth? Give their composition. What is the Enamel? Describe the Cement.
240. Describe the walls of the Pharynx.

241. Name and describe the coats of the Œsophagus.
242. Describe the coats of the Stomach.
243. What is said of the coats and muscular fibres of the intestines? What are the Valvulæ Conniventes? Describe the Villi.
244. How many coats has the Liver? Describe the lobules. What is the mid-vein? What relation the hepatic system to the portal?
245. Describe the coats of the Spleen.
246. What is the Peritoneum?

§ 21. *Chemistry of the Digestive Organs.*

247. What secretions effect chemical changes during digestion?
248. What is Mucus? Its composition?
249. Describe Saliva. Its composition. What is said of it when first secreted? What salts does it contain? State its chemical effect.
250. What are the properties of Gastric Juice? Name its characteristic constituent What saline matter? What of its solvent power? What changes does it effect?
251. Describe Bile. Its composition. What changes caused by it.
252. What is said of the Pancreatic Juice? What per cent. solid matter? Its salts? Its chemical power?
253. Speak of the Intestinal Juices.
254. State the summing up of the changes in three staminal principles of food.
255. What is the relation of acid and alkali in the digestive fluids?

§ 22. *Physiology of the Digestive Organs.*

256. What change in food is necessary? What is Primary Assimilation? What Secondary? What is Digestion?
257. To what is the alimentary canal likened? How is Chyme produced?
258. Speak of the changes of food in the stomach. Can the food return to the œsophagus? Why not? When does the food leave the stomach? What is there peculiar about the Pylorus?
259. What changes occur in the alimentary canal?
260. What becomes of the nutritious part of the food?

§ 23. *Hygiene of the Digestive Organs.*

261. Name the first requisite for the preservation of the Teeth. What is the effect of sudden changes of temperature? Should acids be used? What objection to the use of tobacco? Why should the teeth be frequently examined?

262. When should the temporary teeth be removed? What do the irregular permanent teeth generally require? Does toothache always indicate a necessity of extraction? Observation.

263. What is required for the health of the Digestive Organs?

264. What is said of the quantity of food?

265. What must the supply equal? When must supply exceed waste?

266. When should the quantity of food be diminished?

267. Why is more food required in winter than in summer?

268. To what should the amount be adapted?

269. What should be the quality of food?

270. What must proper aliment contain?

271. How should food be cooked? What are the best methods of preparation?

272. To what should the quality be adapted?

273. What is said of vegetable diet?

274. Who require stimulating food? Who unstimulating?

275. What is said of the manner of taking food?

276. Why should food be properly masticated?

277. Why not take drink with food?

278. Why should regard be had to the temperature of drink?

279. How and when should food be taken?

281. State the reason for not taking food just before or after exercise. What is the influence of moderate exercise? Observation.

282. Why is it not best to eat immediately before retiring to sleep?

283. What influence does the mind exert upon the digestive organs? How should indigestion arising from nervous prostration be treated?

284. After long abstinence, what kind of food should be taken?

285. What influence does the condition of the skin exert?

286. Why is pure air necessary? General Observation. Recapitulation.

§ **24.** *Comparative Splanchnology.*

287. What is said of the Nutritive Apparatus of Vertebrates?
288. Compare the mouth and teeth of the Vertebrates.
289. Of Birds.   290. Of Reptiles.   291. Of Fishes.
292. How are the digestive fluids supplied?
293. Speak of the stomach and intestines of Vertebrates.
294. Give the process of digestion in Ruminants.
295. Name and describe the stomachs of Birds.
296. Compare the alimentary canal of Reptiles with that of Mammals or Birds.
297. What is said of the alimentary canal in Fishes?

UNIFIC REVIEW.

[Compare 225–227 with 287–291.]
Compare the teeth of man with those of the lower animals

[Compare 228 with 292.]
Describe the Salivary Glands in all animals.

[Compare 229–236 with 293–297.]
Contrast the Digestive Organs of Man with those of other Mammals, Birds, Reptiles and Fishes.

[Compare 237, 238 with 36–44, 289–292, 547 and 548.]
Give a full description of the lining membrane of the mouth and alimentary canal of the different classes of animals.

[Compare 239 with 288–291.]
Speak of the difference of the form of the teeth in animals.

[Compare 240–243 with 293–297.]
Give the comparative Histology of the Œsophagus, Stomach and Intestines.

[Compare 244 with 292, 296 and 297.]
What is said of the Liver in the different animals?

[Compare 247–255 with 45–51, 57–60, 65 and 67–70.]
Give an outline of the Chemistry of the Digestive Organs.

[Compare 256–260 with 294 and 295.]
Compare the digestive processes in different classes of animals.

[Compare 280–286 with 209–214, 410–415 and 500–506.]
In what condition should the system be to take food without injury?   State the influence of exercise upon digestion.   What does the health of the human system require?

FIG. 199.   FIG. 200.

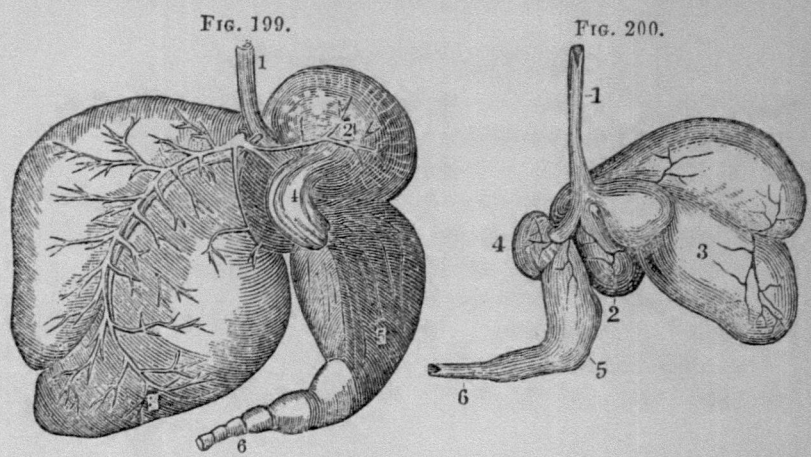

FIG. 199. STOMACH OF AN OX.—1, Œsophagus. 2, Rumen (paunch). 3, Reticulum (honeycomb). 4, Omasum (many-plies). 5, Abomasum (rennet). 6, Intestine.
FIG. 200. STOMACH OF A SHEEP.—1, Œsophagus. 2, Rumen. 3, Reticulum. 4, Omasum. 5, Abomasum, or rennet. 6, Intestine.

FIG. 201.   FIG. 202.

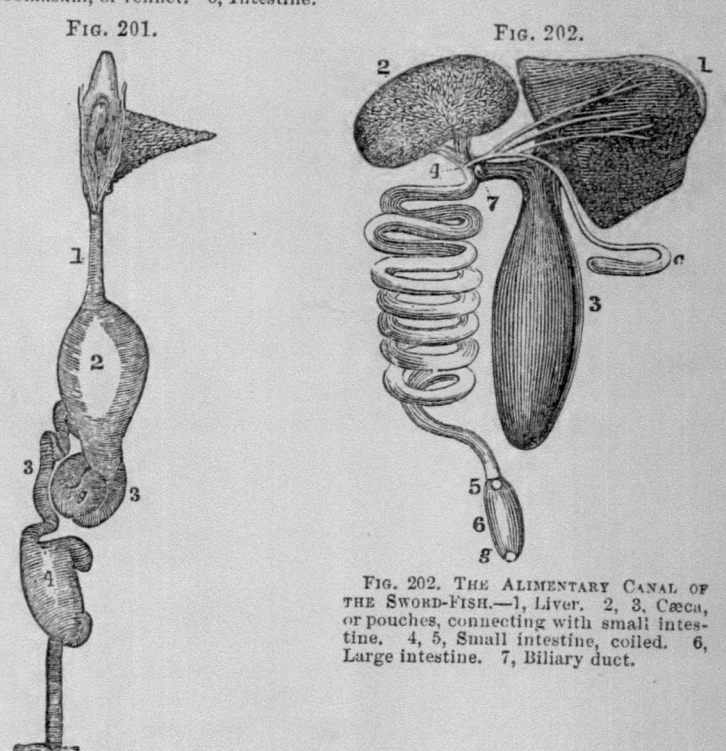

FIG. 202. THE ALIMENTARY CANAL OF THE SWORD-FISH.—1, Liver. 2, 3, Cæca, or pouches, connecting with small intestine. 4, 5, Small intestine, coiled. 6, Large intestine. 7, Biliary duct.

FIG. 201. THE ALIMENTARY CANAL OF THE FLYING LIZARD.—1, Œsophagus. 2, Stomach. 3, 3, Small intestine. 4, Large intestine.

SYNTHETIC REVIEW.

Mouth,
Teeth,
Salivary Glands,
Pharynx,
Œsophagus,   § 19.
Stomach,   *Anatomy of.*
Intestines,
Liver,
Pancreas,
Spleen.
Lining membrane of Alimentary Canal,
    "   "   Mouth,
Composition of the Tongue,
        "   "   Teeth,
Palates,
Pharynx,   § 20.
Coats of the Œsophagus,   *Histology of.*
    "   Stomach.
    "   Intestines,
    "   Liver,
    "   Spleen,
Peritoneum.   CHAP. VI.
Secretions, Names,   *Digestive*
    "   Character,   *Organs.*
Mucus,
Saliva,
Gastric Juice,   § 21.
Bile,   *Chemistry of.*
Pancreatic Juice,
Intestinal Juice,
Changes in Food,
Acids and Alkalies.
Assimilation,
Chymification,   § 22.
Chylifaction,   *Physiology of.*
Destination of Chyle,
Preservation of Teeth,
Removal   "   § 23.
Quantity of Food,   *Hygiene of.*
Quality   "
Manner of taking Food,
Condition of the System,
Nutritive Apparatus of Vertebrates,   § 24.
Mouth and Teeth,   *Comparative*
Digestive Fluids,   *Splanchnology*
Stomach and Intestines.   *of.*

State the Anatomy, the Histology, the Chemistry, the Physiology and the Hygiene, Human and Comparative, of the
Digestive Organs, figs. 199, 200, 201, 202, 203, 204.

    3 *

Fɪɢ. 203.   Fɪɢ. 204.

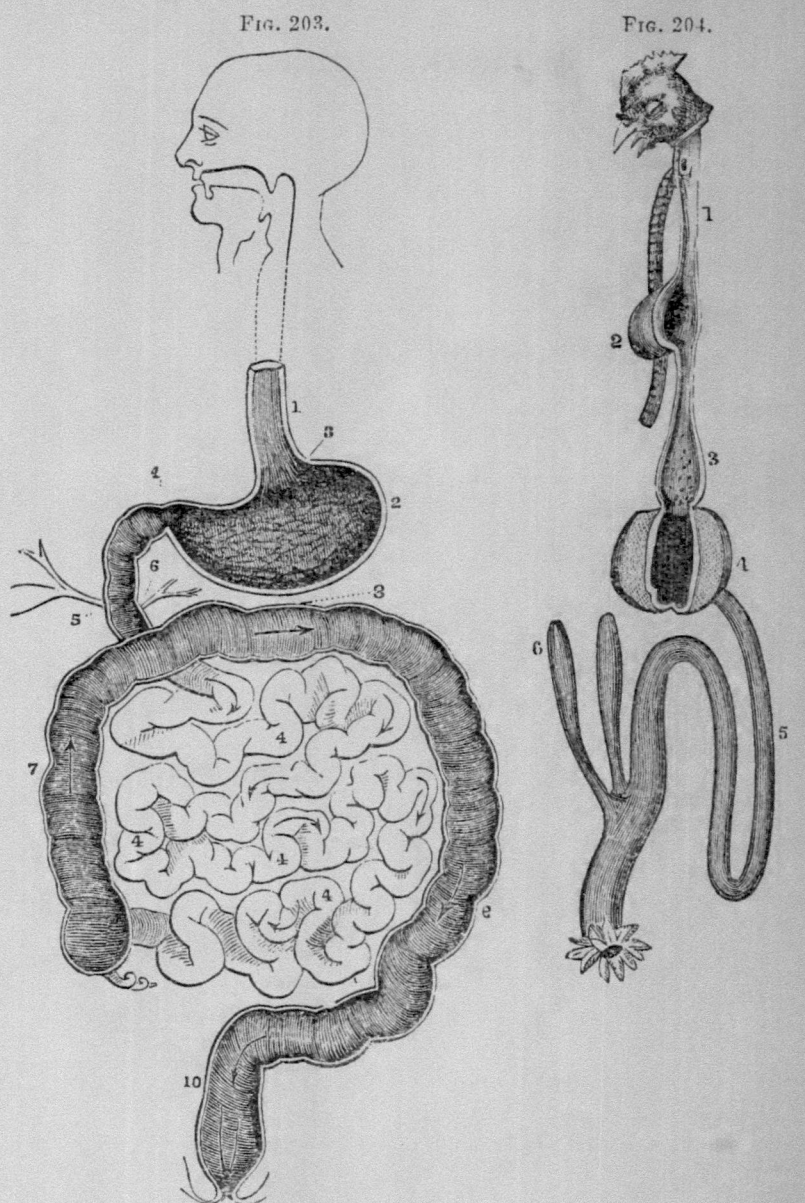

Fɪɢ. 203. Tʜᴇ Aʟɪᴍᴇɴᴛᴀʀʏ Cᴀɴᴀʟ ᴏғ Mᴀɴ.—1, Œsophagus. 2, The stomach. 3, Car-
diac orifice. 11, Pylorus. 5, Biliary duct. 4, 4, 4, 4, Small intestines. 6, Pancreatic
duct. 7, Ascending colon. 8, Transverse colon. 9, Descending colon. 10, Rectum.

Fɪɢ. 204. Tʜᴇ Aʟɪᴍᴇɴᴛᴀʀʏ Cᴀɴᴀʟ ᴏғ ᴀ Fᴏᴡʟ.—1, The œsophagus. 2, Ingluvies (crop).
3, Proventiculus (secreting stomach). 4, Triturating stomach (gizzard). 5, Intestine
6, Two cæca.

ANALYTIC EXAMINATION.

CHAPTER VII.—ABSORPTION.

298. Define Absorption and Absorbents. State the difference between general and intrinsic absorption.

§ 25. *Anatomy of the Absorbents.*

299. Of what do the Absorbents consist? What is Lymph? Describe the Lacteals.
300. What is said of the Lymphatic Glands?
301. Where are the Lymphatic Vessels found? State the kinds of Lymphatics.
302. Give the course of the Thoracic Duct.
303. Describe the Lymphatic Duct.
304. Where are the Lymphatic Glands found?
305. What is the Portal Vein?

§ 26. *Histology of the Absorbents.*

306. Describe the coats of the Lymphatic Vessels. With what are the larger Lymphatic Tubes supplied?
307. What is the supposed composition of the Lymphatic Glands?
308. Give the origin of the Lymphatics and Lacteals.
309. Of what does Lymph consist?

§ 27. *Chemistry of the Absorbents.*

310. What chemical changes occur in the absorbent system?
311. Give the proportions of the chief ingredients of Chyle in the afferent Lacteals. In the efferent Lacteals. In the Thoracic Duct.
312. What changes take place in the Portal circulation?

§ 28. *Physiology of the Absorbents.*

313. What is the office of the Lymphatics?
314. What may the office of the Lymphatics include? What is said of disintegration of the tissues?
315. Speak of the absorbing power of the mucous membrane.
316. Illustrate the absorbent power of the skin.

317. When are the fluids of the serous and synovial membranes absorbed? Observations.
318. Describe Endosmosis.

§ 29. *Hygiene of the Absorbents.*

319. What should be the condition of the air?
320. What influence has moisture?
321. What is the influence of nutritious food upon absorption?
322. What care is necessary in handling poisons?

Fig. 205.

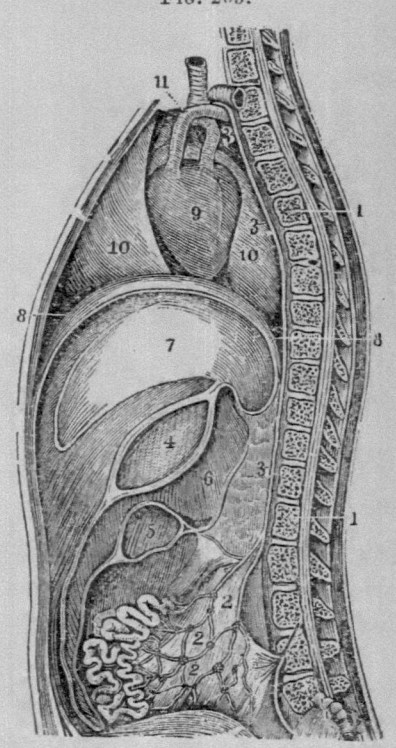

FIG. 205.—Small intestine. 2, 2, 2, Lacteals. 3, 3, 3, Thoracic duct. 4, Stomach. 5, Colon. 6, Pancreas. 7, Liver. 8, 8, Diaphragm. 9, Heart. 10, 10, Lungs. 11, Large vein into which the thoracic duct opens. 12, 12, Spinal column.

SYNTHETIC REVIEW.

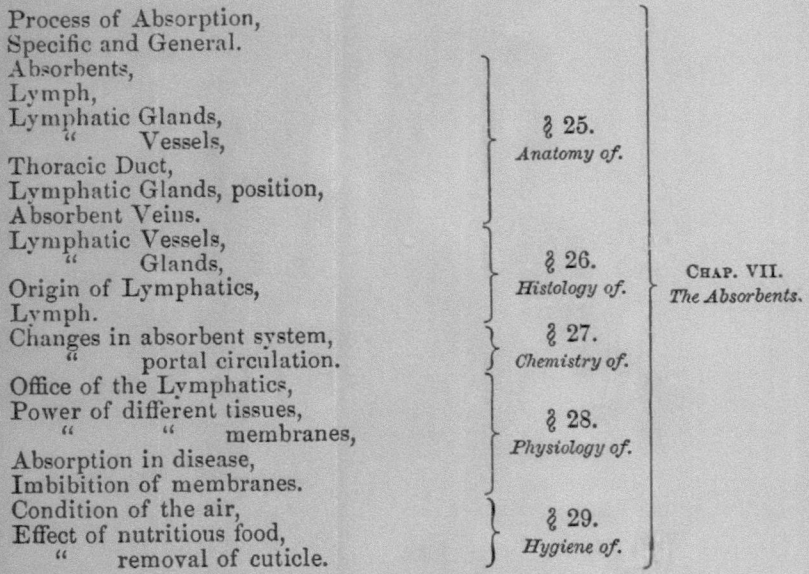

Process of Absorption,
Specific and General.
Absorbents,
Lymph,
Lymphatic Glands,
　　"　　Vessels,
Thoracic Duct,
Lymphatic Glands, position,
Absorbent Veins.
Lymphatic Vessels,
　　"　　Glands,
Origin of Lymphatics,
Lymph.
Changes in absorbent system,
　　"　　portal circulation.
Office of the Lymphatics,
Power of different tissues,
　　"　　"　　membranes,
Absorption in disease,
Imbibition of membranes.
Condition of the air,
Effect of nutritious food,
　　"　　removal of cuticle.

§ 25.
Anatomy of.

§ 26.
Histology of.

§ 27.
Chemistry of.

§ 28.
Physiology of.

§ 29.
Hygiene of.

CHAP. VII.
The Absorbents.

Give the Anatomy, the Histology, the Chemistry, the Physiology and the Hygiene of the Absorbent System of man.

B *

Fig. 206

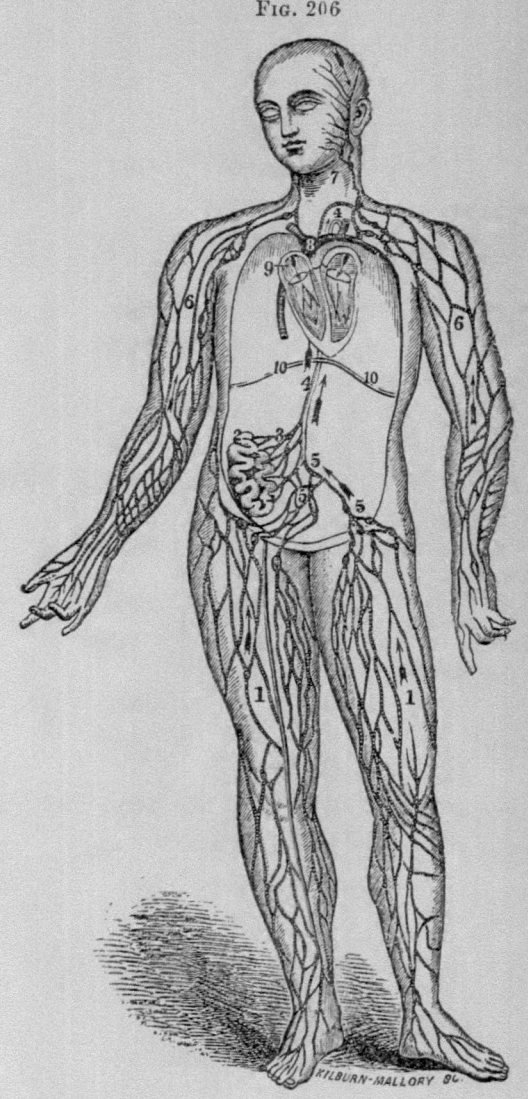

Fig. 206.—1, 1, The absorbents of the lower extremities. 2, The small intestine. 3, The lacteals. 4, 4, The thoracic duct. 5, 5, 5, Absorbent ducts. 6, 6, Absorbents of the arms. 7, Absorbents of the neck. 8, A large vein that opens into the right auricle of the heart. 9, The right auricle. 10, 10, The diaphragm.

ANALYTIC EXAMINATION.

CHAPTER VIII.—THE CIRCULATION.

§ 30. *The Blood.*

323. From what source is the blood derived? Of what does the blood consist?
324. For what purpose is the blood constantly undergoing loss? Observation.
325. Why must the blood be kept in circulation? Name the Circulatory Organs.

§ 31. *Anatomy of the Circulatory Organs.*

326. Describe the Heart.
327. What are the Arteries? To what is the Aorta likened? What are the Capillaries? Where found?
328. Give the course of the Veins. What constitutes the Systemic circulation? What the Pulmonic?
329. From what part of the heart arises the Aorta? Name its divisions. Describe the Arch.
330. State the course of the Thoracic Aorta.
331. What is said of the Abdominal Aorta, its divisions and sub-divisions?
332. Give the divisions of the Carotid arteries. To what parts of the body do the subclavian arteries furnish branches? What is said of the extension of the subclavian artery?
333. How are the Veins arranged? Describe the Superior Vena Cava. Inferior Vena Cava. Portal vein. Pulmonary veins.

§ 32. *Histology of the Circulatory Organs.*

334. Of what is the Pericardium composed?
335. What can you say of the Endocardium? Where does the fibro-elastic tissue form four rings? What and where are the Semi-lunar valves?
336. Where are the Mitral valves? Where the Bicuspids?
337. Upon what is the muscular structure of the heart based? What is said of the superficial fibres? Where is the middle stratum of fibres found?
338. Of what do the muscular fibres of the auricles consist?

339. Name and describe the coats of the arteries.
340. How are the veins constructed? Describe the valves in the veins. Where found?
341. Give the structure of the Capillaries.

§ 33. *Chemistry of the Blood.*

342. State the analysis of the blood.
343. What per cent. of solid matter and water in the blood?
344. How are the mineral substances distributed in the blood? What effect has air on blood?

§ 34. *Physiology of the Circulatory Organs.*

345. Why is circulation necessary? Why a double heart?
346. Give the Systemic circulation; the Pulmonic.
347. What is said of the contraction and dilatation of the auricles and ventricles? What is the effect of such action?
348. In the construction of the circulatory system, what was necessary?
349. By what means are proper circulatory impulses given?
350. How is a backward flow from the auricles prevented? From the ventricles? From the arteries? From the Pulmonary artery?
351. How are the arteries protected against sudden action of the heart?
352. How is the current maintained?
353. Explain the capillary circulation; also the portal current.
354. How is a continuation of the flow through the veins effected?
355. How is the intermittent pressure caused by the action of the heart equalized?
356. What secures the relative amount of blood to each organ?
357. What provision is there for contingencies?
358. By the study of circulation what effect is produced upon the susceptible mind?

§ 35. *Hygiene of the Circulatory Organs.*

359. What temperature should be preserved?
360. Why should the clothing be worn loosely?
361. What is the influence of exercise on circulation?
362. What is said of the quality and quantity of the blood? Illustration.

363. In case of hæmorrhage from divided arteries, what should be done?
364. In flesh wounds, what course is to be taken? Observation. What is the treatment of wounds caused by blunt instruments? Of wounds from poisonous bites?

§ 36. *Comparative Angiology.*

365. What is said of the blood and circulatory organs of Mammals?
366. Of Birds? 367. Of Reptiles? 368. Of Fishes?

UNIFIC REVIEW.

[Compare 323 with 313–318 and 256–260.]

Give in full the change in food during primary assimilation.

[Compare 324 with 369–378.]

How does the blood contribute to the growth of the different parts of the body?

[Compare 325 with 326–333.]

Name and describe the organs by which the blood effects this contribution.

[Compare 326 with 365, 367 and 368.]

Compare the heart of man with that of other Mammals, and with those of Birds, Reptiles and Fishes.

[Compare 327–333 with 365–368.]

Describe the blood-vessels in the different classes of animals.

[Compare 359–362 with 201, 202, 211–214, 264–274, 509 and 591–607.]

What conditions favor free circulation? What can you say of the food in this connection? How is exercise essential to the health of the nervous tissue? In connection with circulation, what is said of the clothing and bathing?

4

SYNTHETIC REVIEW.

Blood, its circulation,
"   loss of,
Circulatory Organs.
} § 30.
    The Blood.

Heart,
Arteries,
Capillaries,
Veins,
Aorta, Arch,
"   Thoracic,
"   Abdominal,
Arteries, Carotid and Subclavian.
Veins, arrangement,
Superior Vena Cava,
Inferior   "
Portal Vein,
Pulmonary Vein.
} § 31.
    Anatomy of.

Pericardium,
Endocardium,
Valves of the heart,
Muscular structure of the heart,
Arteries, their coats,
Veins,   "
Capillaries.
} § 32.
    Histology of.

Analysis of the blood,
Distribution of mineral substances.
} § 33.
    Chemistry of.

Necessity of double circulation,
Systemic Circulation,
Pulmonic Circulation,
Their relation to each other,
Necessary provisions,
Circulatory impulse,
Prevention of the flow,
Current maintained,
Flow through the capillaries,
"   "   veins,
Equalization of the current,
Due supply to each organ,
Provision for contingencies,
Mechanism of the body.
} § 34.
    Physiology of.

Conditions favoring free circulation,
Treatment of divided arteries.
} § 35.
    Hygiene of.

Blood and blood-vessels of Mammals,
"   "   Birds,
"   "   Reptiles,
"   "   Fishes.
} § 36.
    Comparative Angiology of.

CHAP. VIII.
The Circulatory Organs.

Give the Anatomy of the several parts of the Circulatory System, Human and Comparative, the Histology, the Chemistry, the Physiology and the Hygiene.

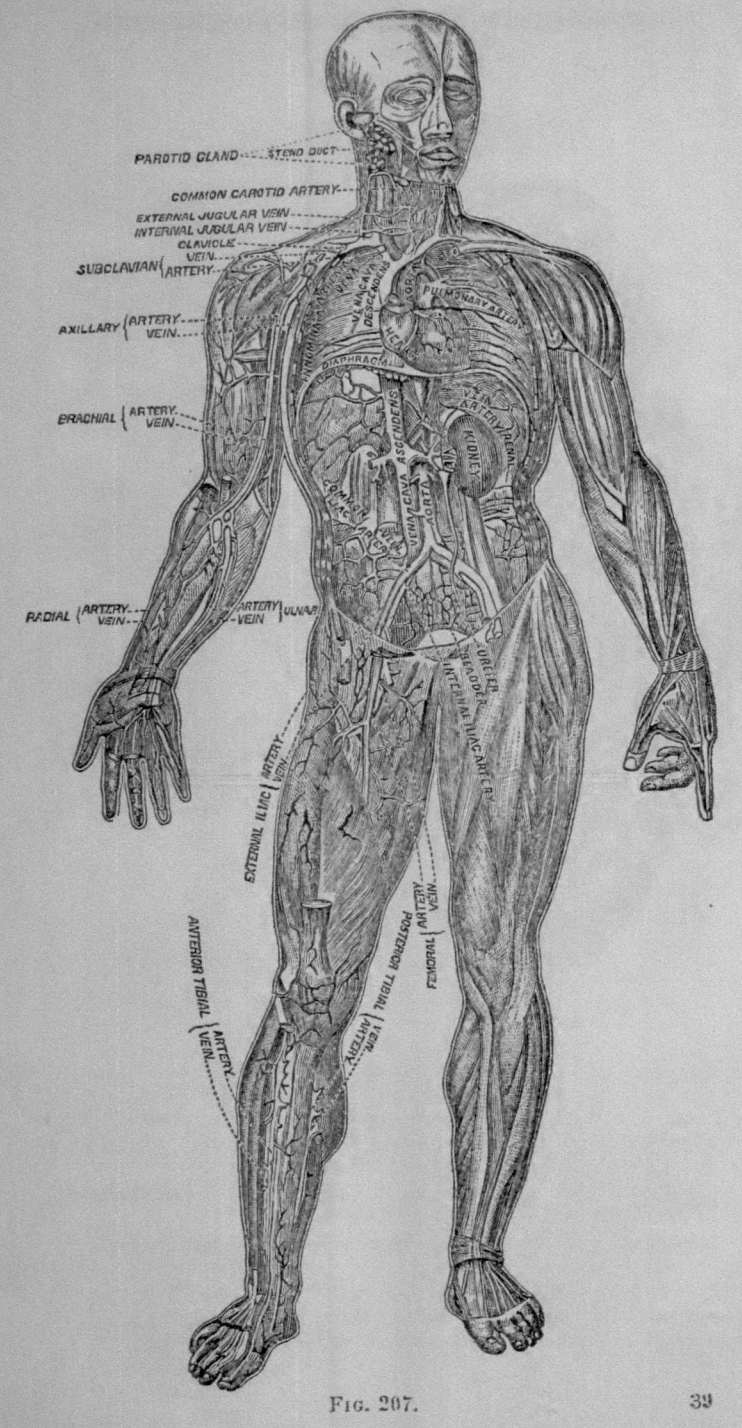

FIG. 207.

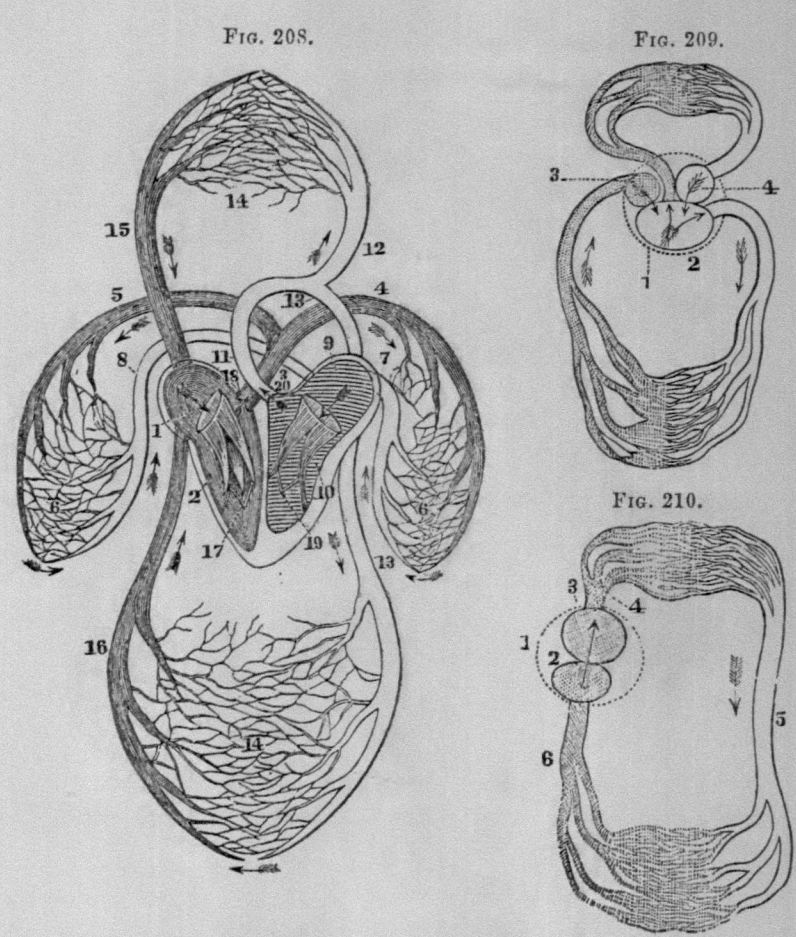

FIG. 208.

FIG. 209.

FIG. 210.

FIG. 208. A DIAGRAM OF THE CIRCULATION OF MAMMALS.—1, Right auricle. 2, Right ventricle. 9, Left auricle. 10, Left ventricle. 4, 5, Pulmonary arteries. 7, 8, Pulmonary veins. 11, 12, 13, 13, Aorta and its branches. 6, 6, Pulmonary capillaries. 14, 14, Systemic capillaries. 17, Tricuspid valves. 19, Mitral valves. 18, 20, Semilunar valves of the pulmonary artery and the aorta.

FIG. 209. A DIAGRAM OF THE CIRCULATION OF REPTILES.—1, The pericardium. 2, The ventricle. 3, The right auricle. 4, The left auricle.

FIG. 210. A DIAGRAM OF THE CIRCULATION OF FISHES.—1, The pericardium. 2, The ventricle. 3, The auricle. 4, The vessel that conveys the blood to the branchia (gills). 5, The vessel that conveys the blood from the gills to the body of the fish. 6, The vessel that conveys the blood from the body of the fish to the heart.

In these three diagrams the arrows indicate the direction of the blood.

ANALYTIC EXAMINATION.

CHAPTER IX.—ASSIMILATION.

§ **37.** *Assimilation, General and Special.*

369. How is life maintained? Distinguish between General and Special Assimilation.
370. What is said of the corpuscles of the blood? What of the blood-plasma?
371. State the first stage in the nutrition of the organs and tissues. What is the second? The third? The fourth? The fifth?
372. How are new cell-elements reproduced? When does this process occur?
373. What is Special Assimilation?
374. Name the secreting glands and membranes. What is said of substances not found in the blood?
375. How is excretion effected? Name the excretory organs. How are the substances which are eliminated from the blood in excretion produced?
376. Speak of the secretory and excretory processes.
377. Describe the kidneys. Observation.

UNIFIC REVIEW.

[Compare 369 with 3.]

In studying assimilation, with what distinctions between organized and unorganized bodies do you become acquainted?

[Compare 370 with 256–260.]

Give the successive stages in Primary Assimilation.

[Compare 371, 372 with 13–17, 45, 46, 119–121, 173, 178, 180, 181 and 460.]

Speak of the structure of cells, and tell how their growth is promoted.

[Compare 373, 374 with 247–255 and 36–44.]

Name the secretory organs, and state the changes caused by their secretions.

[Compare 375–379 with 13, 14, 247, 251, 253, 391–395 and 554.]

Distinguish between Excretion and Secretion. In what processes do the epithelial cells become ruptured? Of what advantage is excretion?

4 *

SYNTHETIC REVIEW.

Assimilation, General and Special,
Blood, its formation,
Assimilation, Secondary, First Stage,
     "   "   Second "
     "   "   Third "
     "   "   Fourth "
     "   "   Fifth "
Secretion,
     "   its glands and membranes,
Excretion,
Secretory and excretory process compared,
Kidneys.

§ 37.
Assimilation, General and Special.

CHAP. IX.
Assimilation.

State what you know of Assimilation, general and special, Secretion and Excretion.

FIG. 211.

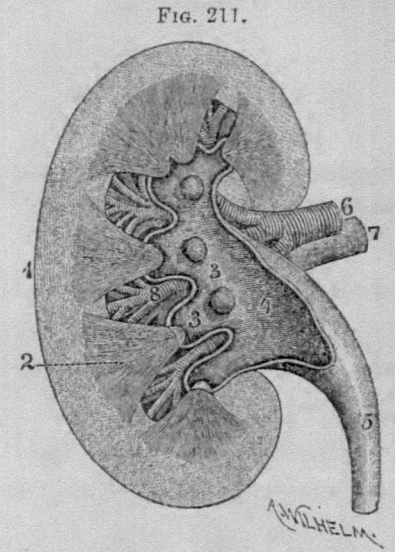

FIG. 211 (*Leidy*). LONGITUDINAL SECTION OF A KIDNEY.—I, Cortical substance. 2, Renal pyramid. 3, Renal papillæ. 4, Pelvis. 5, Ureter. 6, Renal artery. 7, Renal vein. 8, Branches of the latter vessels in the sinus of the kidney.

ANALYTIC EXAMINATION.

CHAPTER X.—THE RESPIRATORY AND VOCAL ORGANS.

§ 38. *Anatomy of the Respiratory and Vocal Organs.*

380. Of what do the Respiratory and Vocal organs consist?
381. Describe the Larynx. Of what is it composed? What is said of the Thyroid cartilage? Of the Cricoid? Of the Arytenoid? Of the Epiglottis?
382. What is the Trachea?
383. Give the divisions and subdivisions of the Trachea.
384. Of how many divisions do the Lungs consist? Of what form are they? What is the Pleura? Compare the Lungs.

§ 39. *Histology of the Respiratory and Vocal Organs.*

385. What is said of the structure of the Larynx?
386. Describe the Vocal cords.
387. Of what is the Trachea made up? Speak of each part.
388. Distinguish between the Bronchi and Trachea.
389. How are the Lungs constructed? In what way are the air-cells connected together?
390. Describe the Pleura.

§ 40. *Chemistry of the Respiratory and Vocal Organs.*

391. Of what does Respiration consist?
392, 393. State the source of carbonic acid.
394. Give the proportions of oxygen and carbonic acid in the arterial and venous blood.
395. State the physical process by which an exchange of oxygen and carbonic acid in the capillaries is effected, also the chemical process.
396. In what respect does expired air differ from that inspired?
397. What is the source of animal heat? Of what temperature the tissues? Of what the blood?

§ 41. *Physiology of the Respiratory and Vocal Organs.*

398. What are the objects of Respiration? What are the results of the chemical changes?
399. Of what acts does respiration consist? How is inspiration effected? Give the motion of the ribs and diaphragm.

400. What is said of the movements in expiration? What muscles are called into action?
401. Define abdominal and pectoral respiration.
402. How is the air in the air-cells renovated?
403. Is the amount of air taken in and given out in respiration always the same?
404. Speak of the frequency of respiration.
405. What are the actions of sighing, yawning, sobbing, laughing, coughing and sneezing?
406. What is the office of the Larynx in respiration? Of what is the Larynx the special organ?
407. What laws govern the vibrations of the vocal cords?
408. What modify the tones? How further modified? Upon what does the general strength of the voice depend?

§ **42.** *Hygiene of the Respiratory and Vocal Organs.*

409. Why is proper respiration important?
410. Why must there be a constant and sufficient supply of pure air?
411. What is the influence of carbonic acid?
412. Mention its sources.
413. What regard should be had for the surroundings of our dwelling-houses?
414. Where is the chief danger?
415. What remarks as to the necessity of ventilation of school-rooms? Of churches?
416. Of concert-halls?
417. State the influence of habit in accustoming ourselves to foul air.
418. What is said of the ventilation of sleeping-rooms? Observations.
419. What attention should be paid to the sick-room?
420. Speak of the means of ventilation in summer.
421. What means in winter?
422. What is the healthiest known means for ventilating a small room?
423. What is said of the use of stoves?
424. Give the quotation on the use of steam for warming rooms.
425. What besides purity of air is required for proper respiration? What objectionable fashion is noticed?
426. Compare the custom of the Chinese women with that of the American.

427. What effect has compression of the mother's chest on her offspring?

428. How can the chest made small by compression be enlarged? Observation.

429. By what is respiration much influenced?

430. State the process of resuscitating persons asphyxiated from drowning, strangulation, electricity, or breathing poisonous gases. Observation.

§ 43. *Comparative Pneumonology.*

431. How does the Respiratory apparatus in all the mammalia compare with that in man?

432. Describe the Lungs of Birds.

433. What is said of the Ultimate Pulmonary Capillaries?

434. What marked modification of respiration in Birds?

435. Speak of respiration in Reptiles.   436. In Fishes.

437. Describe the Gills.

438. What remarkable feature in the organization of some fish?

UNIFIC REVIEW.

[Compare 380–389 with 431–438.]

Compare each respiratory organ in man with that of the lower classes of animals.

[Compare 385–388 with 21, 22, 23 and 25.]

Name the tissues found in the organs of respiration.   How disposed?

[Compare 389 with 26, 36, 37 and 341.]

What tissue in the Lungs?   Describe the variety of Epithelium in the organs of respiration, and name those organs.   Describe the capillaries, and state their relations to the air-cells of the lungs.

[Compare 390 with 39.]

What membrane forms the Pleura?   What is said of it and its secretion?

[Compare 391–396 with 45, 46, 50 and 70–72.]

Give the chemical changes which occur during respiration.

[Compare 397, 398 with 182, 186 and 187.]

What chemical actions produce heat?   State the influence of respiration on motion.

[Compare 425–428 with 206.]

Of what advantage is exercise of the lungs?   What is necessary after exercise?

[Compare 429 with 211, 215, 509, 514 and 515.

What connection is there between respiration and mental energy?   What caution is given?

SYNTHETIC REVIEW.

Larynx,
"   its parts,
Trachea,
Bronchi,
Lungs.
} § 38.
Anatomy of.

Larynx,
Vocal Cords,
Trachea,
Bronchi,
Lungs,
Pleura.
} § 39.
Histology of.

Respiration,
Carbonic Acid,
Exchange of Oxygen and Carbonic Acid,
Expired and inspired air,
Animal heat.
} § 40.
Chemistry of.

Object of respiration,
Modes   "
Renovation of air in air-cells,
Amount of air in respiration,
Number of respirations,
Modifications of respiratory movements,
Double function of the Larynx,
Special   "   "
Vibration of the Vocal Cords,
Conditions affecting tones,
"   "   strength of voice.
} § 41.
Physiology of.

Importance of proper respiration,
Pure blood, how obtained,
Carbonic Acid, its influence,
"   its sources,
Dwelling-houses, location,
"   impure air in,
Public Buildings, ventilation,
Sleeping-rooms,   "
Sick-rooms,   "
Pure air and warmth, how obtained,
Importance of moisture,
Compression of respiratory organs,
Enlargement of the chest,
Influence of nervous system,
Resuscitation of asphyxiated persons.
} § 42.
Hygiene of.

Mammalia, Respiratory Organs of,
Birds,   "   "
Reptiles,   "   "
Fishes,   "   "
} § 43.
Comparative Pneumonology of.

CHAP. X.
The Respiratory and Vocal Organs.

Give the Anatomy, the Histology, the Chemistry, the Physiology and the Hygiene, Human and Comparative, of the Organs of Respiration, figs. 212, 213, 214, 215, 216.

FIG. 212.

FIG. 213.

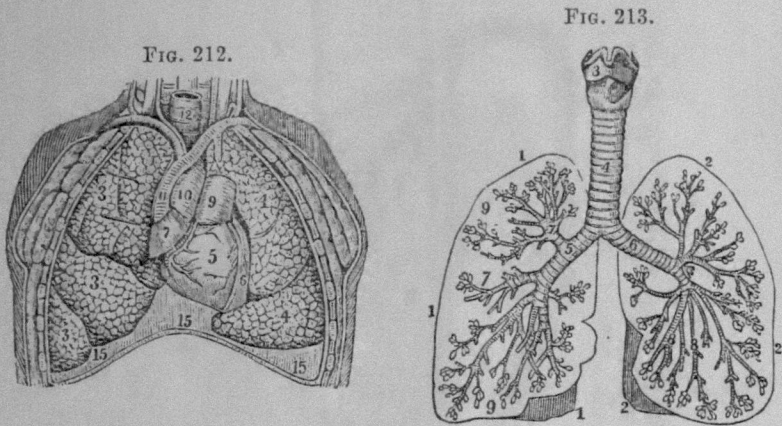

FIG. 212. 3, 3, 3, The lobes of the right lung. 4, 4, The lobes of the left lung. 5, 6, 7, The heart. 9, 10, 11, The large blood-vessels. 12, The trachea. 15, 15, 15, The diaphragm.
FIG. 213. 1, Outline of right lung. 2, Outline of left lung. 3, 4, Larynx and trachea. 5, 6, 7, 8, Bronchial tubes. 9, 9, Air-cells.

FIG. 214.

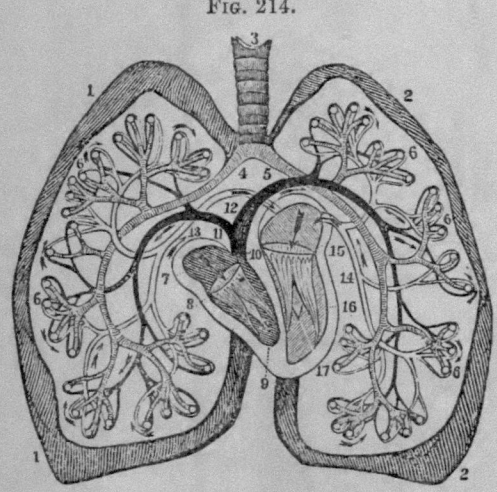

FIG. 214. AN IDEAL VIEW OF THE PULMONIC CIRCULATION.—1, 1, The right lung. 2, 2, The left lung. 3, The trachea. 4, The right bronchial tube. 5, The left bronchial tube. 6, 6, 6, 6, Air-cells. 7, The right auricle. 8, The right ventricle. 9, The tricuspid valves. 10, The pulmonic artery. 11, The branch to the right lung. 12, The branch to the left lung. 13, The right pulmonic vein. 14, The left pulmonic vein. 15, The left auricle. 16, The left ventricle. 17, The mitral valves.

FIG. 215.

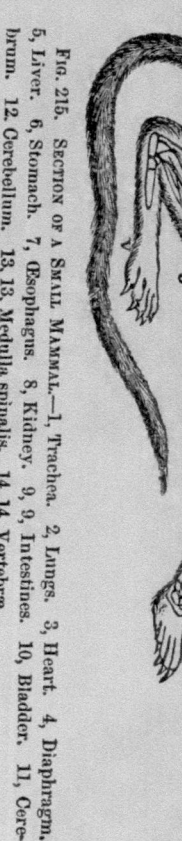
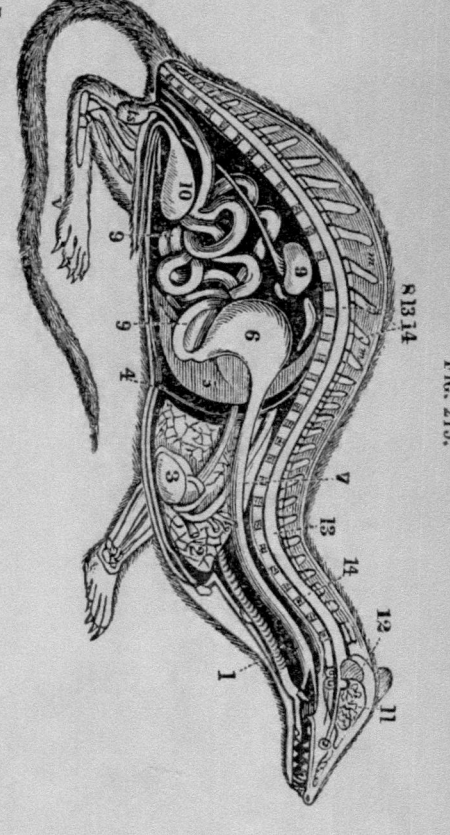

FIG. 215. SECTION OF A SMALL MAMMAL.—1, Trachea. 2 Lungs. 3, Heart. 4, Diaphragm. 5, Liver. 6, Stomach. 7, Œsophagus. 8, Kidney. 9, 9, Intestines. 10, Bladder. 11, Cerebrum. 12. Cerebellum. 13, 13, Medulla spinalis. 14, 14, Vertebræ.

FIG. 216.

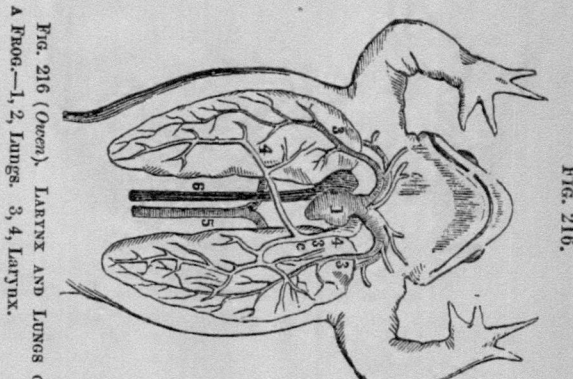

FIG. 216 (Owen). LARYNX AND LUNGS OF A FROG.—1, 2, Lungs. 3, 4, Larynx.

DIVISION III.—THE NUTRITIVE APPARATUS.

SYNTHETIC REVIEW.

SECT. 19. Anatomy of.
" 20. Histology of.
" 21. Chemistry of. } CHAP. VI. *The Digestive Organs.*
" 22. Physiology of.
" 23. Hygiene of.
" 24. Comparative Splanchnology of.

" 25. Anatomy of.
" 26. Histology of.
" 27. Chemistry of. } CHAP. VII. *The Absorbents.*
" 28. Physiology of.
" 29. Hygiene of.

" 30. The Blood.
" 31. Anatomy of.
" 32. Histology of.
" 33. Chemistry of. } CHAP. VIII. *The Circulation.*
" 34. Physiology of.
" 35. Hygiene of.
" 36. Comparative Angiology of.

" 37. Assimilation, General and Special. } CHAP. IX. *Assimilation.*

" 38. Anatomy of.
" 39. Histology of.
" 40. Chemistry of. } CHAP. X. *Respiratory Organs.*
" 41. Physiology of.
" 42. Hygiene of.
" 43. Comparative Pneumonology of.

Division III. *Nutritive Apparatus.*

Give succinctly the Anatomy, the Chemistry, the Physiology and the Hygiene, Human and Comparative, of the Nutritive Apparatus.

DIVISION IV.—SENSORIAL APPARATUS.

ANALYTIC EXAMINATION.

CHAPTER XI.—NERVOUS SYSTEM.

§ **44.** *Anatomy of the Nervous System.*

439. What two formal characters does Nervous Tissue present? Give the arrangement and names of each.

440. How are the Ganglia, Nerves and Commissures arranged? What is included in each system?

441. Describe the Spinal Cord. What is the Medulla Oblongata? To what is this enlargement due? What may be seen in each of the lateral halves of the Medulla Oblongata? What forms the Decussation of the Anterior Pyramids? How is the Fourth Ventricle formed?

442. Where is the Cerebellum? How is the Pons Varolii formed? Describe the Inferior Peduncles of the Cerebellum. What are the Peduncles of the Cerebrum, and why so called? Give the course of these bundles. How are these ganglia connected with the Spinal Cord? Of what does the Quadrigeminal Body consist?

443. What is said of the connections of all the above-mentioned ganglia?

444. How are the hemispheres of the Cerebrum united? How are the ventricles formed?

445. Are the above-mentioned all the ganglia, membranes and galleries which exist in the brain?

446. What is the relation of the Cerebrum to the other parts? How many lobes has each hemisphere? How does the surface appear?

447. How do the convolutions in the two hemispheres compare? What is a remarkable fact respecting these convolutions?

448. What is said of the Cerebellum?

449. What do the brain and spinal cord constitute?

450. Into what classes are the nerves divided? How are the motor and sensory tracts formed?

451. Distinguish between cranial and spinal nerves.

452. Give the grouping and arrangement of the cranial nerves.

453. How many pairs of spinal nerves? How do they differ from the cranial as to their origin?
454. What are the divisions of the spinal nerves? What are plexuses? Name them, and give their formation.
455. Describe the Sympathetic System.
456. What is a peculiarity of the sympathetic nerves?

§ 45. *Histology of the Nervous System.*

457. Name the elements of nervous tissue.
458. Describe the nerve-cells. Where found?
459. Of what do the White Fibres consist?
460. Where are the nerve-filaments distributed? What is said of their individuality? How are they arranged? What their mode of termination?
461. Where are the Tubular Fibres found? What of their size?
462. What are the Gray Fibres?
463. Name the membranes of the Cerebro-spinal System. Describe the Dura Mater, Pia Mater and Arachnoid Membrane.
464. Give a further description of the Dura Mater.
465. What is the Ependyma?

§ 46. *Physiology of the Nervous System.*

466. What opinions have men in different ages held respecting the relation of soul and body?
467. How is the Nervous System related to the compound nature of man?
468. What influence has this system on the different organs?
469. Speak of the connection between the Nervous Centres and the motor and sensitive fibres.
470. Classify the Nervous Centres.
471. Give a full description of the relations existing between the different Centres.
472. What is the function of the Sympathetic Centres?
473. What is said of their connections?
474. Name and illustrate the different kinds of reflex action.
475. Give a marked peculiarity of the Sympathetic System. Illustrate it by the iris of the eye.
476. What is the office of the white substance of the spinal cord? What that of the gray?
477. How is reflex action acquired? State the theory of acquired reflex action as respects repetition.

478. Mention the influence of association. Why is such an arrangement wise?
479. Describe the Sensational Centres. Show that these centres have an independent reflex action. Can they acquire reflex action?
480. What theory is applicable to these centres?
481. How are these centres excited to action?
482. What power have the Ideational Centres?
483. Upon what depends the character of ideas?
484. What is the first way in which the independent reflex action in these centres is manifested? What the second? Third? Fourth?
485. Of what are these centres the seat?
486. What relation is there between the centre of idea and volition?
487. What is the highest energy of which these centres are capable?
488. Upon what does the power of the Will depend?
489. What relations to the Emotions does the Will sustain?
490. What does a free action of the Will require?
491. What influence has the body over the thoughts, emotions and volitions? How does the theory already given find application here?
492. Where does the character of a man leave visible tracings?

§ 47. *Hygiene of the Nervous System.*

493. Why is a knowledge of the laws of the hygiene of this system important?
494. What agencies affect the health of this system? Name the requirements of its health and vigor.
495. What in addition to the features of parents do children inherit? May acquired habits be transmitted?
496. What history is given by M. Morel?
497. What is said of the evil effects of tobacco?
498. What is the effect of all vices in parents?
499. What results spring from nervous diseases in parents? How can such natural constitutions be improved?
500. State the second requirement of health and vigor.
501. Speak of the evil of breathing impure air.
502. What are the results of improper diet?
503. Speak of the effects of alcohol, opium, etc.

504. How does the use of opium compare with that of intoxicating drinks?
505. What is said of the use of tobacco, tea and coffee?
506. What will a want of physical exercise produce?
507. Speak of the benefits of sleep, and the amount needed.
508. Name the third requirement of health.
509. Why is mental exercise essential?
510. Give the remarks of Dr. Ray. What is said of steady employment?
511. Where are seen the saddest effects of an absence of stated employment? What remarks as to the little accomplishments of needlework?
512. To what should the amount of exercise be adapted? What differences are there in the quality of different brains?
513. What is the present tendency in education?
514. State the effect of intense activity.
515. Give the influence of recreation and amusement. Observation.
516. What is essential to the highest mental vigor? What is said of the use of the imagination?
517. What attention is it important to pay to the æsthetic faculty?
518. What is the moral faculty? Upon what depend the happiness and destiny of man?
519. Give Dr. Ray's remarks concerning the hygienic influence of a harmonious development of the mental powers.

§ 48. *Comparative Neurology.*

520. In what respects does the Nervous System of man differ from that of the lower orders of animals?
521. Compare the brain of other Mammals with that of man.
522. Compare that of Birds.
523. Of Reptiles.
524. What is said of the relative size of the Cerebrum? Of the Cerebellum, Medulla Oblongata and some of the organs of Special Sense?
525. Speak of the spinal cord and nerves.
526. Describe the brain of the Fish.
527. Describe the Torpedo.
528. Describe the Electric Eel. What is said of the structure and nervous system of the Articulata? What of them in the Centipede?

5 *

529. Speak of the nervous system in Mollusks.
530. Describe the nervous system in Radiata.
531. How is stimulus received in the lowest forms of animals?
How is it perceived? As we ascend in the animal kingdom, what tissue appears first? What is the simplest
type? Of what do the relations of the animal kingdom
afford an evidence?

UNIFIC REVIEW.

[Compare 439–456 with 520–530 and 471, 472.]
Compare the Nervous System in man with that in the lower orders of
animals.

[Compare 457, 458 with 10, 31, 32 and 36–38.]
Give the composition of Nervous Tissue. Describe its first element.

[Compare 459–462 with 33, 34 and 35.]
Describe the White and Gray Fibres. Where are they found?

[Compare 463–465 with 21, 22, 36, 37, 38 and 39.]
What membranes belong to the Cerebro-spinal System? What names do
they assume there?

[Compare 469–474, 479 and 482 with 441, 442, 446, 455 and 456.]
Name the Nervous Centres. Give their functions. What do they com-
prise?

[Compare 500–502 with 264–279 and 409–412.]
What is essential to the health of the nervous system? What is said of
food and air in this connection?

[Compare 506 with 200–215.]
What can you say of the influence of physical exercise on the health of the
nervous system?

SYNTHETIC REVIEW.

Nervous Tissue. Forms,
 " " Arrangement,
Ganglia, Nerves and Commissures,
Spinal Cord,
Medulla Oblongata,
Cerebellum, Peduncles,
Cerebrum, "
Corpora Striata,
Optici Thalami,
Corpora Quadrigesima,
Corpus Callosum,
Ventricles,
Cerebrum Hemispheres,
Convolutions,
Cerebro-Spinal Nerves,
Cranial Nerves,
Spinal Nerves,
Sympathetic System.
} § 44. Anatomy of.

Nervous Tissue, Composition,
Nerve-Cells,
Nerve-Fibres,
Membranes,
} § 45. Histology of.

Man's compound nature.
Nervous System. Its relation to this nature,
 " " Its rank,
Nervous Centres. Function,
 " " Classes,
 " " Arrangement,
Organic Centres. Function,
 " " Connection,
 " " Modes of reflex action,
 " " Marked peculiarity,
Reflex Centres. Function,
 " " Acquired action,
 " " Importance of acquired action,
Sensational Centres. Character and action,
 " " How excited to activity,
Ideational Centres. Function,
Different persons have different ideas,
Ideational Centres. Independent reflex action,
 " " Emotional character,
 " " Volitional,
Relation of the Emotions to the Will,
Free action of the Will,
Influence of the body for good or evil,
Language of the muscles.
} § 46. Physiology of.

Agencies affecting the health,
Natural heritage,
Impure Air, influence of,
Improper Diet,
Poisons,
Physical Exercise, want of,
Sleep,
Mental Exercise,
Employment,
Amount of exercise,
Intense Activity,
Recreation,
Each faculty to be educated,
The Æsthetic faculty,
The Moral "
} § 47. Hygiene of.

Mammals, Nervous System,
Birds,   "
Reptiles,   "
Fishes,   "
Mollusks,   "
Radiata,   "
Lower forms of Life, "
} § 48. Comparative Neurology of.

CHAP. XI. Nervous System.

C *

Fig. 217.   Fig. 218.

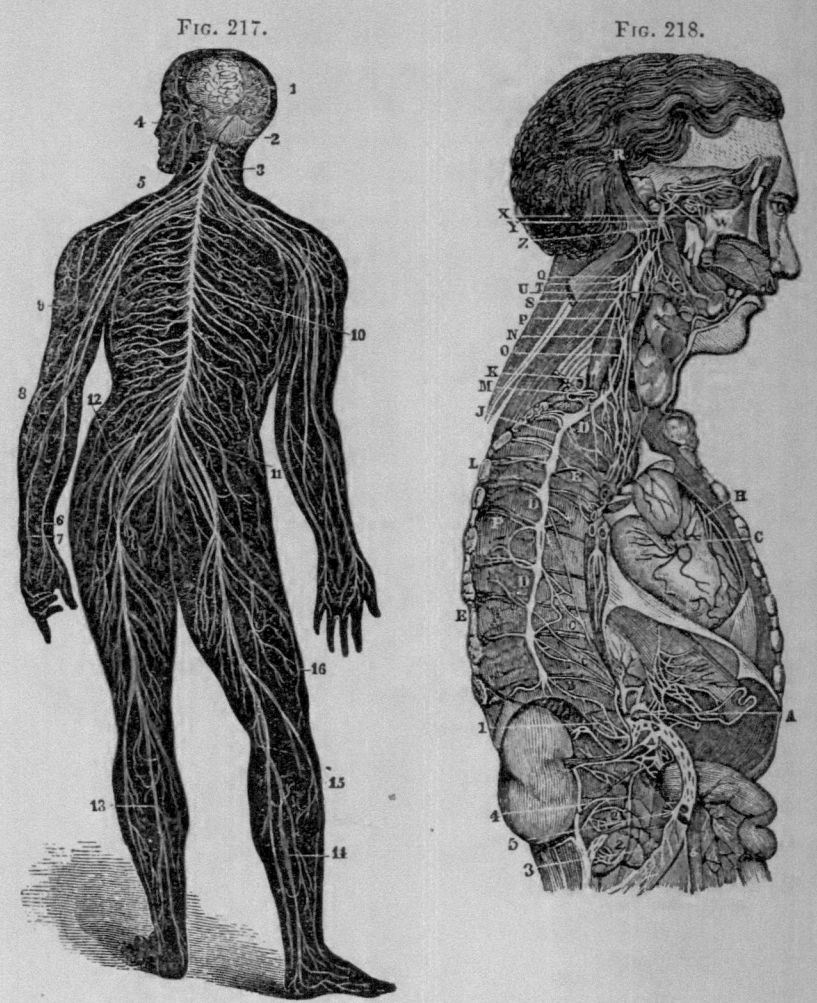

FIG. 217. A BACK VIEW OF THE BRAIN AND SPINAL CORD.—1, The cerebrum. 2, The
cerebellum. 3, The spinal cord. 4, Nerves of the face. 5, The brachial plexus of nerves.
6, 7, 8, 9, Nerves of the arm. 10, Nerves that pass under the ribs. 11, The lumbar plexus
of nerves. 12, The sacral plexus of nerves. 13, 14, 15, 16, Nerves of the lower limbs.

FIG. 218 REPRESENTS THE SYMPATHETIC GANGLIA, AND THEIR CONNECTION WITH OTHER
NERVES, from the grand engraving of Manec, reduced in size. A, A, A, The semilunar
ganglion and solar plexus, situated below the diaphragm and behind the stomach. This
ganglion is situated in the region (pit of the stomach) where a blow gives severe suffer-
ing. D, D, D, The thoracic (chest) ganglia, ten or eleven in number. E, E, The external
and internal branches of the thoracic ganglia. G, H, The right and left coronary plexus,
situated upon the heart. I, N, Q, The inferior, middle and superior cervical (neck) ganglia.
1, The renal plexus of nerves that surrounds the kidneys. 2, The lumbar (loin) ganglion.
3, Their internal branches. 4, Their external branches. 5, The aortic plexus of nerves
that lies upon the aorta. The other letters and figures represent nerves that connect
important organs and nerves with the sympathetic ganglia.

Fig. 219.

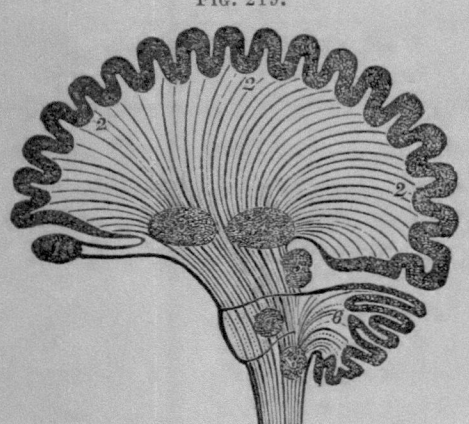

Fig. 219. Diagram of Human Brain, in Vertical Section, showing the situation of the different ganglia and the course of the fibres. 1, Olfactory ganglion. 2, Hemisphere. &, Corpus striatum. 4, Optic thalamus. 5, Tubercula quadrigemina. 6, Cerebellum. 7, Ganglion of tuber annulare. 8, Ganglion of medulla oblongata.

Fig. 221.

Fig. 220.   Fig. 222.

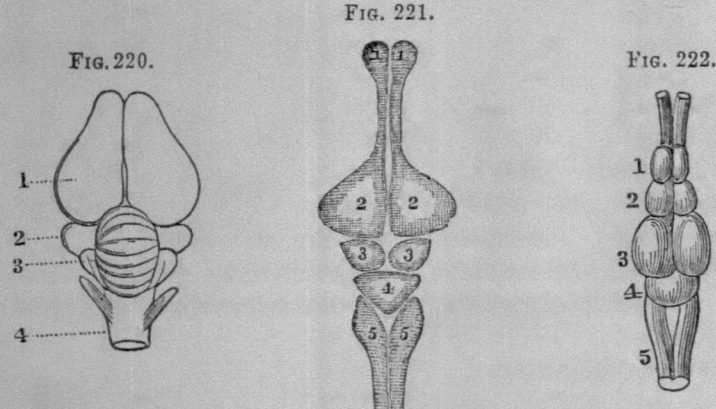

Fig. 220. Brain of a Bird.—1, Cerebrum. 2, Optic ganglion. 3, Cerebellum. 4, Medulla oblongata.

Fig. 221. Brain of an Alligator.—1, Olfactory ganglia. 2, Cerebrum. 3, Optic ganglia. 4, Cerebellum. 5, Medulla oblongata and spinal cord.

Fig. 222. Brain of a Fish.—1, Olfactory ganglia. 2, Cerebrum. 3, Optic ganglia. 4, Cerebellum. 5, Medulla oblongata and spinal cord.

ANALYTIC EXAMINATION.

CHAPTER XII.—The Organs of Special Sense.

§ **49.** *The Anatomy of the Organs of Special Sense.*

532. What is the organ of the sense of Taste? Give a description of the Tongue. From what nerves are filaments received?

533. Describe the organ of the sense of Smell. Mention the nerves.

534. What is the Eye? Name its parts. Of what service is the Sclerotica? Describe the Choroidea. What is its composition? Of what do the ciliary processes consist? What is said of the Iris? What is the Retina?

535. Describe the Aqueous Humor. Crystalline lens. Observation.

536. What is the Vitreous Humor? Distinguish between it and Aqueous Humor.

537. Speak of the muscles of the Eye. Observation.

538. What are the Orbits? Eyebrows? Eyelids? Give the Observation. Of what does the Lachrymal Apparatus consist? Where is the Lachrymal Gland situated? Describe the Lachrymal Canals. Nasal Duct.

539. What is said of the sense of Hearing?

540. Why the Labyrinth so called? Give its divisions.

541. Describe the Vestibule.

542. Describe the Semicircular Canals.

543. Speak of the Cochlea. Of the Fenestra Ovalis.

544. What is the Tympanum? Why called the Drum? Where is the Eustachian Tube? What are found in the tympanic cavity?

545. Describe the External Ear.

546. What is concerned in the Sense of Touch? Give its layers.

547. What is said of the Skin and its connection with the mucous membrane?

548. Give the relation of the Epidermis to the Dermis. What change does the Epidermis experience? What is the seat of color?

549. What is the Cuticle?

550. What is said of the Dermis? What are found with the fibrous and elastic tissues?

551. Describe the Papillæ.
552. Speak of the blood-vessels, nerves and lymphatics of the Cutis Vera.
553. Where are the Hair-Follicles? Describe the different parts of a hair. What results from the contraction of the unstriated muscular fibres?
554. Describe the Oil-Glands.
555. Where are the Sweat-Glands? What are "pores"? What is "insensible perspiration"?
556. Speak of the Nails. Of what is the horny part composed? How do they grow?

§ 50. *Physiology of the Organs of Special Sense.*

557. State the primary use of the sense of Taste. What is said of this sense in man? What is the effect of cultivation?
558. Is the sense of Smell one of great importance? Why not?
559. When light passes through different media, to what changes are its rays subject? What effect has convex or concave surfaces? Illustrate and apply the above principles.
560. Give the shape of those parts of the eye which act as media. State the use of so many lenses.
561. In what case will a more convex and in what a less convex lens be required? How is the eye able to change the convexity of its lenses and vary its focal distances?
562. What is the cause of short-sightedness and long-sightedness? What suggestion in the selection of glasses?
563. What is the function of the Sclerotic coat? What that of the pigment of the Choroid coat? How may the functions of some parts of the eye be beautifully shown?
564. Speak of the accessory parts of the eye. What enables the eye to move without friction? How are the eyelids drawn together? Give the functions of the Eyelashes and Eyebrows.
565. What is Hearing?
566. What is the function of the External Ear?
567. What that of the Auditory Canal? State the design of the Eustachian Tube. Give the uses of the Vestibule, Cochlea and Semicircular Canals.
568. What are distinguished by this sense? How does this apparatus compare with that of vision?
569. Speak of the special organ of the sense of Touch.

570. State the threefold functions of the skin.
571. Give the uses of the Epidermis.
572. How is the Cuticle destroyed and replaced?
573. Of what service are the cutaneous Papillæ?
574. Where does vitality reside? Why there?
575. What power does the surface of the skin possess?
576. What are the uses of the oil derived from the oil-glands?
577. State the uses of Perspiration. By what is the quantity influenced?
578. What is the influence of the condition of the atmosphere?
579. Give the functions of the Hair and Nails.

¿ 51. *Hygiene of the Organs of Special Sense.*

580. What perverts the sense of Taste? By what is this sense varied?
581. By what does the sense of Smell become impaired?
582. What care is necessary in using the eye?
583. What is the effect of sudden transitions of light?
584. What should be avoided?
585. How should the eye of the child be trained?
586. What is beneficial? Observation.
587. Can the sense of Hearing be improved?
588. How may this sense be impaired? Observation.
589. What parts are absolutely essential, and what not?
590. To what must attention be given?
591. What is said of the use of clothing?
592. Of what material should it be? Compare furs, woolen cloth silk, cotton and linen.
593. Why should the clothing be porous and loosely fitted?
594. To what must it be suited? Observation.
595. Who require the more clothing?
596. What is said of clothing when a vital organ is diseased?
597. What persons need less clothing?
598. What is said of cleanliness of the clothing?
599. What of damp clothing?
600. What is indispensable to health?
601. What effect has bathing on the internal organs?
602. State the simplest mode of bathing.
603. Speak of the shallow bath.
604. Upon what must depend the frequency of bathing?
605. What should the time be?

606. In what diseases is bathing of *great* importance?

607. State the rules to be observed.

608. State the influence of pure air.

609. What influence does light exercise?

610. What is a blister? What care should be taken? How is vesication prevented?

611. What are Corns? From what comes the pain?

612. What is said of Frost-bite? How is Chilblain caused?

FIG. 223.

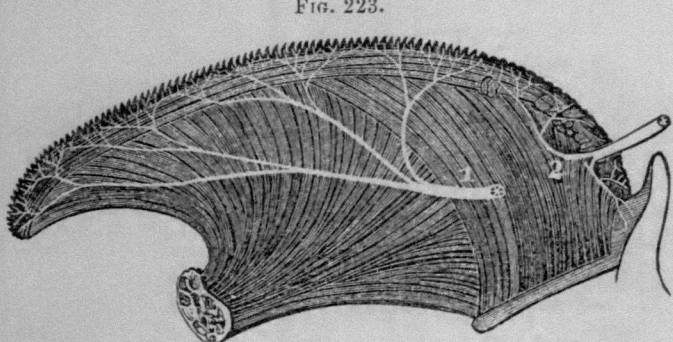

FIG. 223 (*Dalton*). DIAGRAM OF THE TONGUE, with its sensitive nerves and papillæ. 1, Lingual branch of fifth pair. 2, Glosso-pharyngeal nerve.

FIG. 224.

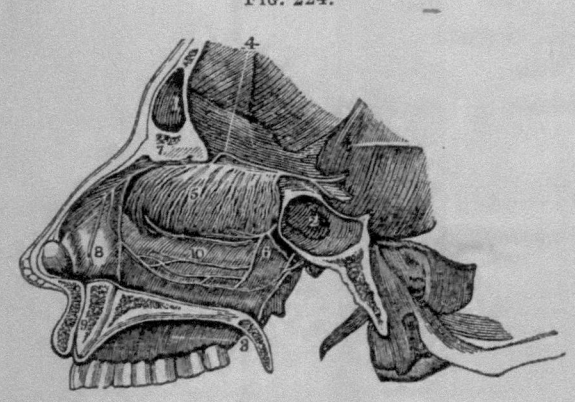

FIG. 224. A SIDE VIEW OF THE PASSAGE OF THE NOSTRILS, AND THE DISTRIBUTION OF THE OLFACTORY NERVE.—4, The olfactory nerve. 5, The fine divisions of this nerve on the membrane of the nose. 6, A branch of the fifth pair of nerves.

6

SYNTHETIC REVIEW.

Organs of Taste, Smell and Sight,
Sclerotica, Choroidea,
Ciliary Processes,
Iris, Retina,
Aqueous, Crystalline and Vitreous Humors,
Muscles of the Eye,
Orbits, Eyebrows, Eyelids,
Lachrymal Glands and Canals,
Nasal Duct,
Organs of Hearing,
Labyrinth, Vestibule,
Semicircular Canals,
Cochlea, Tympanum,
External Ear,
Organs of Touch,
Two layers of skin—Epidermis and Dermis,
Hairs,
Sebaceous and Respiratory Glands,
Nails.

§ 49.
Anatomy of.

Sense of Taste, Primary use,
"   Smell,   "
Laws of Light,
"   Adaptation of the eye,
Short-sightedness, Cause,
Long-sightedness, "
Defect remedied,
Coats, Function,
Accessory parts of the eye,
Hearing,
External Ear, Function,
Auditory Canal, "
Eustachian Tube, "
Cochlea and Semicircular Canals, Function,
Hearing,   "
Organ of Touch,
Skin, Function,
Epidermis and Cuticle, Function.
Cutaneous Papillæ,
Corium, Vessels,
Oil-Glands, Function,
Perspiration. Use,
"   Quantity,
"   External condition,
Hair and Nails.

§ 50.
Physiology of.

CHAP. XII.
The Organs of Special Sense.

Sense of Taste. Perversion,
"   Smell,   "
Eye, how to be used,
Amaurosis,
Oblique positions, long-continued,
Viewing objects at different distances,
Bathing the eye,
Dust, removal,
Defective Hearing, Cause,
Hearing, parts essential,
Clothing, Material,
Class of persons needing more clothing,
Clothing, Cleanliness,
Bathing. Modes,
"   Time,
"   General Rules.
Water a curative agent,
Skin. Air beneficial,
"   Effect of light,
Burns and Scalds, Treatment,
Corns, Frost-Bite.

§ 51.
Hygiene of.

State the Anatomy, the Physiology and the Hygiene of the Organs of Special Sense, the Care of the Sick, of Poisoned Persons and of persons injured in any way.

FIG. 225.

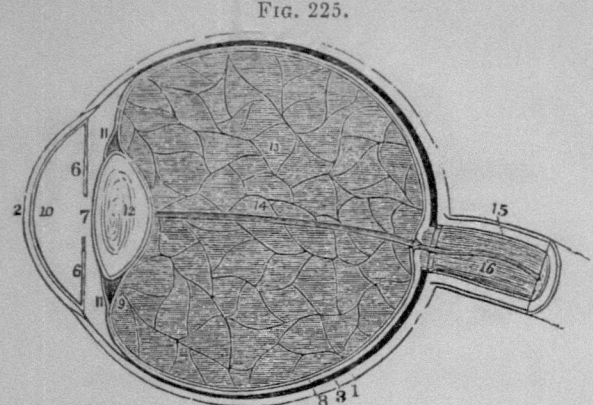

FIG. 225. A SECTION OF THE GLOBE OF THE EYE.—1, The sclerotic coat. 2, The cornea. (This connects with the sclerotic coat by a beveled edge.) 3, The choroid coat. 6, 6, The iris. 7, The pupil. 8, The retina. 10, 11, 11, Chambers of the eye that contain the aqueous humor. 12, The crystalline lens. 13, The vitreous humor. 15, The optic nerve. 16, The central artery of the eye.

FIG. 226.

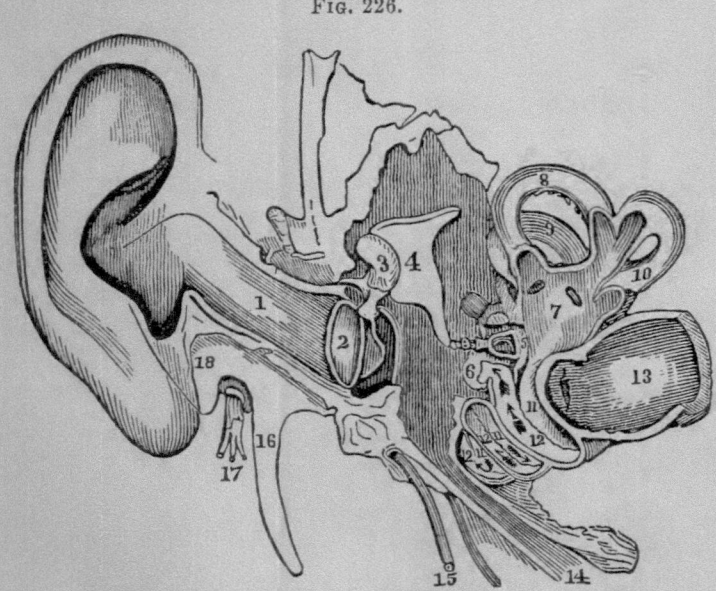

FIG. 226. A VIEW OF ALL THE PARTS OF THE EAR.—1, The canal that leads to the internal ear. 2, The membrana tympani. 3, 4, 5, The bones of the ear. 7, The central part of the labyrinth (vestibule). 8, 9, 10, The semicircular canals. 11, 12, The channels of the cochlea. 13, The auditory nerve. 14, The opening from the middle ear, or tympanum, to the throat (Eustachian tube).

APPENDIX.

CHAPTER XIII.—CARE OF THE SICK.

§ 1. *The Nurse.*

[Compare 591–599.]
Cleanliness.—What regard should be had for cleanliness?

[Compare 601–608.]
Bathing.—Mention what is said respecting bathing.

[Compare 264–286.]
Food and Drink.—What is said of the food and drink of the sick? Name the means of nourishment, and tell how they are prepared.

Temperature.—Speak of the temperature of the sick-room.

Light.—What suggestions are made as to light?

Quiet.—How may quiet be had? Mention other duties of the nurse.

§ 2. *The Watcher.*

Give the duties of the Watcher.

§ 3. *Poisons and their Antidotes.*

When poisons have been taken, what is to be done? Name the most common poisons, and their antidotes.

[Compare 363.]
How can hæmorrhage be arrested?

[Compare 364.]
Give the manner of dressing wounds.

[Compare 430.]
How may asphyxiated persons be recovered?

[Compare 610–612.]
Speak of Burns, Scalds and Frost-Bite, and their treatment.

DIVISION IV.—SENSORIAL APPARATUS.

SYNTHETIC REVIEW.

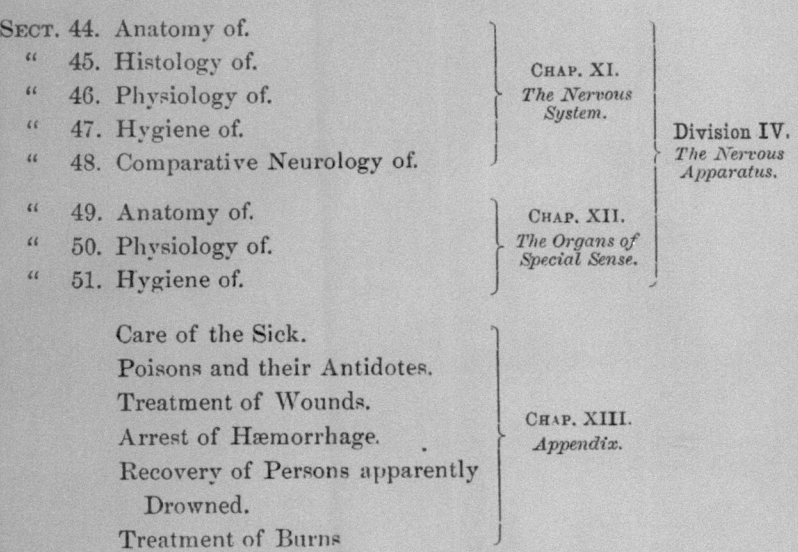

SECT. 44. Anatomy of.
"   45. Histology of.
"   46. Physiology of.
"   47. Hygiene of.
"   48. Comparative Neurology of.

CHAP. XI.
*The Nervous
System.*

"   49. Anatomy of.
"   50. Physiology of.
"   51. Hygiene of.

CHAP. XII.
*The Organs of
Special Sense.*

Division IV.
*The Nervous
Apparatus.*

Care of the Sick.
Poisons and their Antidotes.
Treatment of Wounds.
Arrest of Hæmorrhage.
Recovery of Persons apparently
    Drowned.
Treatment of Burns

CHAP. XIII.
Appendix.

State the Anatomy, the Histology, the Physiology and the
Hygiene, Human and Comparative, of the Nervous Apparatus,
and the Care of the Sick, Poisons and their Antidotes, Treatment
of Wounds, Hæmorrhage, Burns, and persons apparently drowned.

SUMMARY.—SYNTHETIC REVIEW.

SECT. 1. The Three Kingdoms of Nature Compared. " 2. Definitions.	CHAP. I. *General Remarks.*	**Division I.** *Outline Principles.*
" 3. Cells. " 4. Tissues. " 5. Membranes.	CHAP. II. *General Histology.*	
" 6. Solids and Fluids.	CHAP. III. *General Chemistry.*	
" 7. Anatomy of. " 8. Histology of. " 9. Chemistry of. " 10. Physiology of. " 11. Hygiene of. " 12. Comparative Osteology.	CHAP. IV. *The Bones.*	**Division II.** *Motory Apparatus.*
" 13. Anatomy of. " 14. Histology of. " 15. Chemistry of. " 16. Physiology of. " 17. Hygiene of. " 18. Comparative Myology.	CHAP. V. *The Muscles.*	
" 19. Anatomy of. " 20. Histology of. " 21. Chemistry of. " 22. Physiology of. " 23. Hygiene of. " 24. Comparative Splanchnology.	CHAP. VI. *The Digestive Organs.*	
" 25. Anatomy of. " 26. Histology of. " 27. Chemistry of. " 28. Physiology of. " 29. Hygiene of.	CHAP. VII. *The Absorbents.*	
" 30. The Blood. " 31. Anatomy of. " 32. Histology of. " 33. Chemistry of. " 34. Physiology of. " 35. Hygiene of. " 36. Comparative Angiology.	CHAP. VIII. *The Circulation.*	**Division III.** *Nutritive Apparatus.*
" 37. Assimilation, General and Specific.	CHAP. IX. *Assimilation.*	
" 38. Anatomy of. " 39. Histology of. " 40. Chemistry of. " 41. Physiology of. " 42. Hygiene of. " 43. Comparative Pneumonology.	CHAP. X. *The Organs of Respiration.*	
" 44. Anatomy of. " 45. Histology of. " 46. Physiology of. " 47. Hygiene of. " 48. Comparative Neurology.	CHAP. XI. *The Nervous System.*	**Division IV.** *Nervous Apparatus.*
" 49. Anatomy of. " 50. Physiology of. " 51. Hygiene of.	CHAP. XII. *The Organs of Special Sense*	
Care of the Sick. Poisons and Antidotes. Treatment of Wounds, Hæmorrhage, of apparently Drowned Persons and of Burns.	CHAP. XIII *Appendix.*	

Mammals.

State succinctly the Anatomy, the Histology, the Chemistry, the Physiology and the Hygiene of Mammals.